Kamala

Kamala Made Herself Free, Free Like a Bird
She Had No Wings To Fly, She Couldn't Drive a Car
But She Knows How To Push a Pencil

Daisy Mae Spoonamore

1st edition 2025

ISBN Paperback: 979-8-9923404-9-5
ISBN Hardcover: 979-8-9926609-0-6
Library of Congress Control Number: 2025933635

Acknowledgments

If you want to go somewhere in your life; you got to pay the alternated price. I asked, if I could do one-thing and to succeed, at it, what would that be? I always wanted to be one of the best writers of all times in the world I live in. I wanted my writing to be your entertainment; from the beginning, through the middle and would keep readers glued to the book from start to the finish.

In order to do so, I just knew I needed to take a course in Creative writing. So when I did write you the reader could recognize the echo of what went down the road, tracks, river or even what went through the air.

I wanted my writing to have colorful characters by bringing them to life. I wanted a combination of compelling stories. Being a Creative Writer, I would have to know how to know, how to work words, so they could fasten together to create a variety of thinking's; to surprise the reader on what I would write. Two magical words a writer loves for everybody to see **by line** in **bold letters.**

Dedications

I fell, I was blessed with one of the most important person in my life; Ronald L Spoonamore my spouse lacking 4 months and ten days from being 56 years of marriage, until God called him home on March the first 2020; from having Bladder Cancer; gone, but not forgotten. Who has supported me during my journey as a Creative Writer. Ron, I like to take this moment to tell you how much I appreciate for what you; Ron has made it possible so that I could take the Creative Writing Course and, too, "Thanks, Spoonamore, for making it possible so that I could have tools in my kit and necessity supplies so that I could do my works in a masterpiece, yours truly your wife, Daisy Mae.

At this moment, I like to give thanks to Jake Thompson, The Senior Strategist of McMillan Book writing for being very patience with me, in helping me to fill out the necessity papers as a client to The McMillan Book Publishing Service Agreement and application form. Jake, stayed with me from his phone and me on my computer and phone, by constructing me step by step until everything was filled out in a orderly matter, Best Regards, Daisy Mae Spoonamore.

Contents

Introduction of my book, about Kamala

At the age of thirty-seven, Kamala is reconnection with her past through strangers she meets and welcomes into her home. Through the years she had picked up a peculiar habit but uses it to her advantage when faced with emotional situations, A yellow envelope that is handed to her contains photos of these strangers and unfolds with information she needs to carry out her quest for answers. Follow as she establishes herself as a professional writer and earns the qualifications for a coveted award, a prestigious crowning for her efforts.

Jeff

Jeff felt like something was nudging him, he had naught one clue what could be so important in having his morning disturb. He was getting annoyed by this. Jeff went for his second cup of hot steaming coffee. Jeff felt like he was being kicked hard back into the living-room. His eyelashes lead him over to his empty chair.

Jeff had two different thoughts scrambling through his thinkings. While Jeff was doing his usual routine, he asked himself the first thought, then he asked himself the second thought.

CHAPTER ONE

The Letter Holder That Was Filled with Note Pads for Story Ideas

Kamala made herself a prisoner in her own home for twelve years. She loved to write and had written over 1200 fairytales from the note pads that were held in the letter holder from the old desk she'd found. Kamala kept very little communication with the outside world. She was running out of story ideas she needed more material.

Kamala noticed she had gained too much weight throughout that time from eating too much junk food and drinking an abundance of sodas to quench her dry mouth and throat after all she ate that made her mighty thirsty.

Kamala decided to take a break from her typewriter and made herself completely free; free like a bird. She had no wings to fly, she couldn't drive a car but she knew how to push a pencil and she loved to walk just anywhere. She decided she would and Kamala finally set herself free and was on her journey with note pad and pencil to jot down everything she came across that she thought would draw attention of the reader and hold them fast until they came to the end of the story.

She was looking for something or someone that would be more realistic like different people in different relations; to write about their habits and their patterns of behavior and to write the facts that made them the person they were.

Kamala had noticed a particular man and by watching him he looked like he was hungry, lonely, and could use a friend. She

1

approached the stranger and introduced herself, he said nothing but he started to cry. He was holding his face in his grubby hands and started tapping his face with his fingers over and over.

Kamala dared not to ask him anything because he just kept on weeping. She had no words to say but she could feel his pain. She felt helpless as expressions of sadness came across his face. Kamala mustered up enough courage to ask the stranger,

"Are you hungry? I'll buy."

He replied by saying,

"I don't take charity."

Kamala told the stranger with an anxious voice,

"Well that's ok, but I'm hungry too."

Then the stranger said with a smile,

"Let's go get something to eat because my belly tells me it's empty!"

The stranger had a quizzical expression on his face as if he were studying her facial features. He could see she had high brows and high cheek bones. He had an expression on his face as if he wanted to ask Kamala something. She asked him,

"Why are you looking at me that way and why are you so sad?" "What is it that makes you cry like you do?"

The stranger put his grubby hands in his pocket and Kamala jumped back. He said quickly,

"Don't be afraid! I just want to show you a picture!"

Kamala replied,

"Well first let's get something to eat because seriously I'm hungry!"

Kamala and the stranger walked until they came to a diner.

She told the stranger,

"I'm going to the ladies room first."

While she was gone the stranger went to the men's room. When Kamala returned she saw the stranger had his face and hands clean and she couldn't help but to stare at him. He asked her,

"What is it, is there something wrong?"

Kamala responded while moving her head back and forth saying,

"Oh! nothing."

The two took a seat; Kamala asked the stranger with an anxious voice,

"Now let's see that picture you wanted to show me!"

The stranger put his hands in his pocket and pulled out a folded envelope that looked like he had carried it for many years and laid it on the table. He opens it slowly and took the picture out. This was a very intense moment for the stranger when Kamala picked up the faded photo and started looking it over. It was a photo of a pretty little girl. The appearance of the face was a perfect likeness of Kamala with high-brows and high-check bones. Kamala looked at the stranger with a questionable face and asked the stranger,

"Who is she may I ask?"

The stranger asked Kamala with sadness in his voice,

"You don't know, do you? I was hoping that you would."

Kamala kept staring at the little girl's face and ask the stranger with a question,

"Am I supposed to know?"

The stranger told her with an expression of joy on his face,

"She's my daughter!"

3

While Kamala was studying the little girl's face she asked the stranger,

"When was the last time you saw your daughter?"

He took the envelope and showed the date that it had been sent to him. While pointing to the date that was stamped on it he said,

"It was a few days before that date."

Kamala asked the stranger,

"How old was your daughter when this picture was taken?"

The stranger replied,

"She was seven years old."

Kamala calculated the years and said,

"She must be my age by now because the date on that envelope was thirty-years ago and did you say she was seven when that picture was taken right?"

The stranger answered,

"Yes, that's right."

Kamala looked at the stranger and asked him,

"Do you want me to help you find your daughter?"

The stranger had tears rolling down his face and struggled to speak and responded by saying,

"Yes...I would appreciate that young lady, thank you."

Kamala handed the stranger a handkerchief and picked up the picture to take a closer look. She studied the girl's facial expressions. It was like she knew who this little girl was. Then she picked up the envelope and looked at the return address. It had no name just an address. Nothing looked familiar to Kamala here. While she was looking at the photo the stranger started reminiscing about the years he had his daughter were together and hoping that Kamala might say something that would relate to what he was telling her. It was like he knew Kamala. He kept staring at her and she noticed that and asked him,

"Why are you staring at me. Is something wrong?"

He said with assurance,

"There's something about your face. It's telling me something."

After they finished eating the stranger paid for both tabs. The stranger started walking along with Kamala and while they were he started to say something to her. Kamala looked at the stranger with a stunned look. It was like she remembered him!

She said anxiously,

"How horrible of me Daddy, to forget!"

The stranger didn't know what to say. He was lost for words but he started to cry and he put his hands on his face and started tapping his face with his fingers like he did when she had met him. He started to reach for her but Kamala put her arms around the stranger and the two wept together. What a moment for the two of them!

Now Kamala had a story to write. She went home and started typing again. That was the story about............

The Letter Holder That Was Filled With Note Pads For Story Ideas.

CHAPTER TWO

Special Moments

K amala started thinking about the times when her Daddy would take his daily walks and would pass the playground during noon recess at the Elementary School. She cherished those special moments and she looked forward to that every day.

Kamala recalled the special moments when she and her Daddy made cupcakes for her and her classmates to celebrate Kamala's Birthday.

No matter how busy Kamala was she always took time to make her Daddy personalized gifts for every occasion and made unique center-pieces for the kitchen table for every annual event.

Kamala cherished the special moments when she could climb up on her Daddy's lap and he would read her fairytales and he would rock her to sleep.

After seven years had passed her Daddy seemed all of sudden to disappear. She felt heart broken and would ask herself,

"Why isn't my Daddy here anymore?"

Kamala started dwelling on the past thirty years that her Father had been gone. She sat in her rocker hours on end while she lingered over questions she had for her Father. She was wondering why her last name was different than her Daddy's and where has her Daddy been living all those years? Why did he have grubby hands when she found him? Had he been living in the streets if so, why? Did her Daddy try to find her during those years and if not why?

Kamala remembered when she and her Daddy spent time together on Saturday mornings watching cartoons on the TV. Those were very special moments for the two but she thought to herself,

"Those times are gone, or are they?"

Kamala decided to go back out and see if she could find her Father. She didn't want to neglect her Father. She started walking toward the place where she found him earlier. She kept on walking until she saw him standing near a bench it seemed as if he was going to sit down. He noticed her when he turned and ask her,

"Kamala, what are you doing out so late?"

Kamala just stared at her Father with uncertainly about what question she was going to ask him. Instead, he asked her,

"Well child, what is it?"

Kamala didn't know what to say. She just stood there in a frozen state and kept staring at her Father. Then he asked Kamala in an anxious voice,

"Come out with it child! What is it that you're wanting to ask me?"

Kamala started stumbling over her words as if she couldn't ask him anything. Then she said abruptly,

"Daddy, why is it that your last name is different from mine?"

He replied by saying with tears rolling down his face,

"Well, child..."

he stopped.

Kamala asked her Father,

"What is it, Daddy? I can take it. I'm not a little girl anymore, I'm 37 years old now."

Kamala's Father swallowed really hard like he had something in his throat and asked her,

"First Kamala, how about you and I sit down?"

The two sat down on the bench; then her Father said,

"Kamala, it's like this, are you sure you want to know?"

Kamala said to her Father very seriously,

"Of course, I do Daddy, please tell me!"

He started out by saying,

"Your Mother and I weren't married at the time you were born. Back then it was a disgrace to be unwed and pregnant so your Mother was sent away to a home for unwed Mother's but she..."

he stopped......

Kamala told her Father,

"Go on Daddy, I'm listening."

Her Father finished what he was trying to tell Kamala by saying,

"She didn't want to deprive you of her last name. Your Mother wanted you and I to be together but it couldn't happen. I'm sorry child but your Mother did love you very much!"

Kamala said to her Father in a sad tone,

"But Daddy how was it that you got to raise me? Didn't the Mothers have to give up their babies back then?"

Kamala's Father said sadly,

"Yes of course child, that's why your Mother was sent away but I went and got you when I knew the time was right and brought you to raise myself."

Kamala replied by asking her Father,

"Did you steal me, Daddy?"

Kamala's Father answered her by saying,

"Well child, I did but I lived 300 miles from where your Mother and I had lived at the time you were born."

Kamala asked her Father,

"Daddy, why did you all of sudden disappear after my 7th Birthday?"

He answered her in a serious voice,

"The law found out that I had you and where we were living and they took you away from me."

Kamala's Father started crying. Kamala said in an apologetic voice,

"I'm sorry Daddy that I put you through all those questions but I had a need to know."

Kamala's Father assured her by saying after he composed himself,

"That's ok child, you had the right to know."

Kamala asked her Father with a big smile on her face,

"Daddy how about you coming over to my place and I'll cook for us and we can have fun like we used to when it was just the two of us. You don't have any plans, do you?"

Her Father answered her by saying with a smile on his face,

"Kamala I've always loved your smile; And even more now because I have my little girl back; I mean my grown-up child...Yes, let's spend some time together again."

That was the story about........

Special Moments.

CHAPTER THREE

All She Wanted Was Just One Simple Answer

It was day-break when Kamala and her Father got to her home. While Kamala was cooking breakfast for her and her Father she was in deep thought over the one question she had wanted to ask him. She could hear her Father talking but her thoughts were wondering on how he would react to the question she wanted to ask him and not knowing what kind of an answer she would receive.

Kamala set the table, served up the food and took off her apron. Her Father scooted her chair up to the table and then seated himself. Kamala said to her Father,

"Daddy, I hope you brought your appetite because I've cooked up enough food for an army."

He replied by saying,

"It looks delicious child so let's eat!"

After her Father finished eating he gave his approval by smacking his lips.

After breakfast, Kamala and her Father cleaned up the kitchen and she had worked up enough courage to ask her Father that one question that was burning in her thoughts, but before she could even say the first word her Father remembered it was Saturday and said anxiously,

"Turn on the TV Kamala, cartoons are on!"

Kamala procrastinated because she was preoccupied with the thought of asking her Father the one question that had been on her mind throughout her life.

Kamala finally approached her Father with that one question she'd been waiting forever to ask him,

"Daddy, where have you been living the last thirty years?"

Her Father answered in a grunting tone and giving her several answers.

"Well, which one do you want to hear child; the tack room, an old barn, the sleeping cars, or under the bridge?"

Kamala couldn't describe the look she saw on her Father's face then. It was something she had never experienced from him before and said compassionately,

"I do apologize for that Daddy! I'm not prying, all I want is just one simple answer....................."

Her father said loudly and abruptly,

"You can see there's no one simple answer child!"

Her Father started walking toward the kitchen door. She asked him with sadness in her voice,

"Daddy, where are you going? You're not leaving, are you?"

Kamala saw that her Father was getting restless and said, quickly,

"Don't go, Daddy! I don't want to hurt you! I want to help you! You know that I love you! Don't you?"

Kamala paused and added,

"I'm concerned about my Father!"

He answered her roughly,

"Child can't you see your Father is......."

He stopped talking and opened the door to leave. Then Kamala said sincerely,

"Daddy, you don't have to be homeless. You can stay here with me. I have plenty of room for us both."

Her Father turned and said.

"Remember child, as I told you once before, I don't take charity!"

Before Kamala could say,

"It's not charity Daddy, I'm offering you a place to live!"

Her Father turned from her and walked away.

That's the story about……

<u>All She Wanted Was Just One Simple Answer.</u>

CHAPTER FOUR

What Am I Suppose To Do Now?

K amala wasn't going to let that conversation go. She followed her Father and asked herself out loud,

"What am I supposed to do now?"

She thought to herself,

"My day began with me and my Father at my home after thirty years and eating breakfast at my kitchen table and after I asked just one question it ended with him walking out of my life."

Now it was almost as if her Father was hearing her thoughts as he turned around and started walking back toward Kamala's home to tell her how sorry he was to leave like he did. He didn't have to walk very far because she had been right behind him. He said, abruptly and sadly,

"Child, you don't want an old man like me living in your home, do you?"

Kamala looked at her Father with a big smile and said,

"Daddy, the cartoons are still on; how about you and I go back home and watch them?"

and they did.

After the cartoons were over Kamala fixed some homemade vegetable soup and cold cut sandwiches for lunch. It was a pleasant day with the two of them laughing at the cartoons and spending time together in a positive atmosphere.

It was about midnight when Kamala put fresh linens on the bed in the guest room for her Father. Before Kamala's Father went to bed he said,

"Now I need some reading material."

Kamala said as she handed him a book,

"Here Daddy!"

It was one of Kamala's books she had written and she was hoping he would enjoy it. Her Father was impressed by the book jacket and recognized that it had been written by his own daughter. He was very proud and before the two turned in for the night her Father said with a yawn,

"Good night, child."

Kamala likewise said to her Father,

" Good night, Daddy.

That was the story about

What Am I Suppose To Do Now?

CHAPTER FIVE

Daddy Read This One To Me... Please?

When Kamala's Father stepped into the guest room he was intrigued by the number books that lined the book-selves; almost as if he had been introduced to the Library of Congress. He was astonished by what he saw.

He started reading the titles. Some titles sounded vaguely familiar to him. He started going down memory lane to the times when he would read fairytales to Kamala and he could still hear his little girl saying with an anxious voice while holding a fairytale book in her hands,

"Daddy read this one to me........Please?"

He recalled reading some of them at least 100 times or more.

He took one book off the shelf and saw it was written by his grown child Kamala, but the one he had chosen to read was not a fairytale. The title read,

What Would I Do Without You, Daddy?

It brought tears to his eyes. He held the book close to his heart. He composed himself and opened the book to a page that read,

Someday Daddy, you will come back!
He continued with the words that read,
Because I still need you, Daddy.
I still want my Daddy here.
I have lots of memories...
but I need more; without you....
I feel I can't fulfill my dreams....

15

Kamala

I need a rewarding life......
I need to give myself a great gift
or more than what I have.
I feel unique and imaginative.
As myself, I can be more productive.
Daddy, you have given me the reason to write.
Now I have hopes and dreams to share.
What would I do, where would I be if it wasn't for you?
Oh, I have so much to share.........
But as for me and my memories....
Oh, they're always there.
What would I do without you?

Kamala's Father fell quietly to sleep on that thought and slept soundly, until day-break. This is the story about............................

<u>Daddy Read This One To Me Please?</u>

CHAPTER SIX

It's A Good Day To Go Outside And Play

After Kamala's Father read that book of his choice, before going to sleep he felt uneasy about that story and wanted to try to make up for lost time. He did not know that Kamala had washed his garments and had a letter and a photo in her Father's jacket and would have questions for him. Kamala called to her Father,

"Daddy, breakfast is ready! I bet you're hungry, at least I hope you are because there's enough food here for the two of us and then some!"

Kamala's Father jumped and put his slacks and jacket and acknowledged that he knew they had been washed. He had mixed emotions about this whole situation. He went out to the kitchen to join Kamala at the table but before he seated himself he saw the letter and photo lying there. He was apprehensive about that. Kamala noticed her Father eyeing the letter and photo and asked him,

"Daddy, did I do something wrong?"

He replied by saying,

"No child, why?"

Kamala looked at her Father and ask anxiously.

"Daddy who is she?"

He just stared at his daughter like he didn't have an answer. He didn't want to answer because of what he had to tell her and how she might react to it. Kamala blurted out,

17

"Daddy is that young lady my Mother?"

Kamala's Father wasn't up for this challenge and said nothing. But Kamala asked her Father,

"Daddy, why are you trying to ignore me? Remember you're not talking to a child. Please tell me, Is she my Mother?"

Before her Father could even answer Kamala just kept on with one question after another.

"Where is she, Daddy?"

Her Father felt like he had been cornered and it knocked him for a loop. He took a deep breath. It felt like he was going to pass out. Kamala asked her Father in a concerned voice,

"Daddy, are you ok? Can I get you something?"

Her Father had a haggard look on his face after all the questions his daughter had asked. Kamala asked her Father,

"Daddy, we can talk later; let's eat breakfast before it gets cold, ok?"

Her Father replied,

"That's ok child, this is something you should know because she is your Mother."

Kamala picked up the photo and took another look and her Father said,

"Yes, Kamala that is your Mother, she's beautiful, isn't she? You and she have the same smile."

Kamala asked her Father anxiously,

"Daddy where is my Mother, you haven't told me where she is?"

Kamala's Father started crying. Then Kamala asked him sadly,

"Is my Mother dead?"

Her Father was lost in his thoughts and kept weeping. Kamala saw how hurt he was and didn't ask her Father anymore questions. He composed himself and told Kamala sadly,

"Yes! Child she is and I'm sorry to say she was hit by a car and died instantly before I could even say good bye."

Then her Father went on saying,

"The driver was drunk and fled the scene and before you ask me, child, yes he got life in prison."

Kamala asked her Father,

"Where was my Mother laid to rest?"

He replied by saying,

"It's in the same city where your Mother and I met."

Kamala asked him,

"Could we go and see her Daddy?"

Kamala's Father answered her by saying anxiously,

"Of course, we can child!"

Her Father looked at her as if he knew she was going to ask him if they could go today. But instead of waiting for that question he quickly changed the subject and anxiously said,

"It's a good day to go outside and play!"

Kamala snapped at her Father and uttered with angry words,

"Daddy I want to see my Mother!"

Her Father said abruptly,

"I don't think I can go back there, child!"

Kamala said with apologetic voice,

"Sorry Daddy, I didn't mean to come at you like that!"

Kamala's Father said,

"That's ok Kamala, it's my duty to see to your needs and that's one of them. Let's take a bus to the city and go to see your Mother, ok child?"

Her Father finished by saying,

"We can go today if you like."

Kamala and her Father took the bus to the city of Cincinnati to see where her Mother was laid at rest.

The trip was quiet for the two of them. Nothing was asked and nothing was said all the way to the city. But when they got to the grave site they grieved together and Kamala laid some field flowers on her Mother's grave. She and her Father prayed together over it and left silently.

That's the story about.....

It's A Good Day To Go Outside And Play.

CHAPTER SEVEN

Be The Friend You Would Want To Have

When leaving the Baltimore Pike Cemetery where Kamala's Mother had been laid to rest quite a few years back, it was heart wrenching for her because she had no memories of her biological Mother, but it made her feel proud to know she had her Mother's smile. The route the bus driver had taken seemed very familiar to Kamala and when he drove past a housing project called English Woods Kamala told her Father while pointing to the apartments,

"Daddy there's one of the places I lived after I was taken from you."

Her Father asked her,

"Are you sure child?"

She answered by saying,

"Of course, Daddy, I'll never forget that address! That's one place I always loved."

Her Father asked her,

"Do you remember the people that took care of you there?"

Kamala replied anxiously,

"Yes of course I do! She was a loving and caring woman. She told me something very special, I'll never forget the words she said to me before going out to play."

Her Father asks her,

"What was that child?"

Kamala answered her Father by saying,

"Be The Friend You Would Want To Have."

Her Father asked her another question that pertained to that woman,

"By any chance do you remember her name?"

Kamala answered her Father with another question,

"Dottie was her name, Why Daddy?"

Kamala's Father asked her,

"Now Kamala, what was the address where you lived with this loving, caring woman?"

Kamala answered her Father with another question because it seemed as if he was analyzing everything she was telling him;

she answered,

"1981 D Sutter Ave., Why Daddy?"

Kamala proceeded before her Father could even ask her another question and said,

"She was like a friend you would want to have Daddy. But after a few years, I was moved from there and was taken to Camp Washington. By the time I got acquainted with the other children that lived there I was taken far away again and that's how I ended up living close to where I live now."

Then Kamala said,

"Daddy, Dottie was a true friend of mine. I hated leaving her."

Before Kamala could say anything else her Father started to speak but the bus stopped suddenly. It was close to Kamala's home now and so Kamala and her Father walked to the Clertoma Village where she was living. Before they stepped into her home, she looked at her Father in a quizzical manner and her Father asked her,

"What is it, Kamala?"

She replied by saying to her Father,

"Did you know Dottie?"

Her Father just stood still like he had seen a ghost and stared at Kamala's face. It seemed like he wanted to say something, but no words were coming from his mouth. Kamala asked her Father anxiously,

"What is it, Daddy? You're scaring me!"

Kamala's Father started slurring his words and Kamala just knew her Father was having a heart-attack. He kept staring like he was in a trance and Kamala asked her Father again,

"What is it, Daddy? you're scaring me!"

Kamala screamed,

"Daddy you can't leave me, I can't lose my Father, not now!"

Kamala didn't hesitate she helped her Father to the stoop then ran inside and dialed 911. When they responded Kamala told them, frantically,

"My Father's dying, Hurry Please...!"

Kamala felt helpless. Her Father was trying to tell her something with a dire look on his face. Kamala said,

"What is it Daddy that you're trying to tell me?"

The paramedics arrived at the scene in no time and one of them started checking Kamala's Father while the other paramedic questioned her about her Father's health. She knew nothing except his name. Before Kamala could tell her Father's name she drew in a deep breath and let it out slowly and said,

"My Father's name is Jim Jackson, help him please!"

Before she could say anything else the paramedic that was checking her Father looked at Kamala with concern. She just knew he was going to tell her something she didn't want to hear so she went over to her Father and sat down where he was and she held him in her arms. Then the paramedic said to her,

"Madam unfortunately your Father......"

he stopped. Kamala cried out loudly,

"No! Daddy, you can't leave me now. Daddy fight with all you have!"

Kamala felt like her own life was losing its breath...and in a few seconds Kamala hovered over her Father's body and sobbed loudly, crying over and over,

"No Daddy! No Daddy! No! You can't leave me. I can't lose my Father again!"

After a few minutes, both paramedics tried their best to help Kamala up to her feet but she just wouldn't leave her Father's side. The paramedic who had been trying to help her Father told Kamala with a caring voice,

"Sorry madam There is nothing else we can do. We've done all we could to help your Father."

The paramedics helped Kamala up and took her inside her home. One of the paramedics told Kamala the Coroner was on his way to take her Father.

When the Coroner arrived, Kamala opened the door and saw him putting a white sheet over her Father's body. She felt bewildered and collapsed in the paramedic's arms. Then the other paramedic helped him to lay Kamala on the couch.

This was a tragic and intense moment for Kamala. The coroner went inside to ask Kamala a question. One question after another. She felt like she was being interrogated. When the time came for her Father to be taken away she covered her face with her hands and started tapping her fingers on her face like the day she meets that stranger that was now known to be her Father. She felt helpless and sobbed loudly and walked outside to her Father and fell to her Father's side and told him,

"I love you, Daddy!"

The paramedics helped the Coroner put the lifeless body of Kamala's Father into the hearse and they left. The next thing that she remembered was the letter she had found in her Father's jacket and she went to the guest room where her Father had slept to look for it; it was under the pillow her Father had laid his head upon to sleep. She picked up the letter and started to open it. Everything she touched had her Father's scent on it and she laid down on the bed exhausted and cried herself to sleep. That's the story about....

<u>Be The Friend You Would Want To Have.</u>

CHAPTER EIGHT

It's A Ghost Town

Upon wakening Kamala felt unsettled because she couldn't remember why she was sleeping in the guest room. She had never slept there before and she only used that room for storing the books she had written.

Kamala felt frazzled and confused and started to turn over to go back to sleep but she felt the wad of paper in her fist.

After a few seconds, Kamala opened her hand and took the paper out then took both hands to try to smooth out the wrinkles. She tried to read what was written and hoped she could find the reason she had it in her hand in the first place and why she was in that room at all. She tried to read what was written on it but it looked like chicken scratch she thought she may need someone to interpret what was written. Instead, she laid the paper down and left the room.

Kamala went to the kitchen to put on a pot of coffee. While she was waiting for it to perk she went to her bedroom and took a look in the mirror on her vanity. She looked unkempt and decided to take a shower and get dressed for the day. She went back to the kitchen and prepared breakfast. When she was finished she called for her Father, "Daddy I hope you're hungry because I fixed plenty for the both of us and then some!"

Something dawned on her when she didn't hear her Father walking down the hall way to the kitchen. It hit her like she had the wind knocked out of her because all of sudden she remembered dialing 911 and telling the dispatcher anxiously,

"My Father is dying, Hurry please...!"

Kamala felt like a thief had come in the night and had taken her Father away from her. Kamala went back in time when she was taken away from her Father thirty years before. This all felt way too much for her. She had just told her biological Mother good-bye; a Mother she had never known and alas now she was to make funeral arrangements for her Father. But this was something that had to be taken care of.

Kamala didn't have much information about her Father except what she had known of him from the first seven years of her childhood and also, she really didn't have much more than that after finding her Father a few days ago.

All of a sudden Kamala remembered her Father was consistently asking her questions while they were on the bus about the loving and caring 40-year-old woman that had taken care of her when she was taken away from her Father. It was as if he knew her.

Kamala had recurrent thoughts of the letter she was trying to read that very same morning. The address on the envelope had the same address of where she first lived when she was taken away from her Father so long ago. Kamala went to the guest room and picked up the letter and thought just maybe she could find information about her Father, at least a telephone number of this woman, and give her a call. Kamala looked it over and over. It was still unreadable to her but she found a telephone number she recognized.

It was the same number, she remembered while living with Dottie. She said out loud,

"Humm, yes, Hu-19181."

Kamala took her chances and dialed it. She was told by the operator,

"The number you have just dialed is not a working number."

She hung up. Kamala's instincts told her she could catch a bus and try to find Dottie but she didn't think it would be wise to go alone. Kamala remembered a man, not much older than she, waiting for the same bus that her Father and she had taken to the cemetery. She remembered his name and told herself out loud,

"Oh yes; Jeff Johnson! Could he be by any chance be related to Dottie?"

She got a telephone book and looked up his number. She found his name and dialed the number; she was in luck, he answered.

Kamala told him,

"You don't know me but I was hoping you could help me."

He asked Kamala,

"How is that?"

Kamala answered Jeff by asking him,

"By any chance is Dottie Johnson any kin to you?"

He replied by saying with assurance,

"Yes, she is, she's my Mother but what do you need her for?"

Then Kamala told Jeff,

"By the way my name is Kamala Waits and I lived with Dottie thirty years ago in English Woods for a few years until I was taken away from her and lived elsewhere."

Jeff told Kamala.

"My Mother doesn't live in English Woods anymore. No one lives there anymore."

She replied by asking,

"What do you mean no one lives there anymore?"

Jeff answered by saying,

"Well, it's a ghost town, no one has lived there for years."

Kamala asked Jeff,

"Then may I ask; where does Dottie live now?"

He replied,

"You just did; my Mother lives near Camp Washington but why all of the questions?"

Kamala answered Jeff with sadness in her voice,

"My Father..."

then she stopped,

Jeff told Kamala,

"Now Kamala, take a deep breath and tell me, ok?"

She did. Kamala finished what she was trying to tell Jeff;

"My Father had a heart-attack last evening after we came back home from visiting my Mother's gravesite, that's where we were going when we met you on the bus."

Jeff answered with much concern,

"I'm sorry to hear about your Father but what does that have to do with me?"

Kamala told Jeff,

"I believe my Father knew your Mother."

Jeff asks Kamala,

"How is that?"

Kamala said to Jeff,

"Because I have a letter here that belongs to my Father and the return address on the envelope is the same one your Mother lived at when I was with her."

Jeff replied by saying,

"Kamala, I'll be more than happy to help you."

Kamala answered anxiously,

"Thanks, Jeff, I need all the help I can get!"

Not long after that conversation Jeff and Kamala caught a bus to go to see Dottie. Kamala was hoping she could help her. Jeff told Kamala while they were on the bus,

"Kamala, I do remember my Mother having other children living with her but I didn't live there all the time because I lived with my Father. You see, my parents were separated and divorced when I was about eight years old."

When the bus arrived at Dottie's home the two went inside, Jeff called to his Mother and she came out to the living room wearing a robe. Jeff asked his Mother,

"What's wrong Mother are you sick?"

Dottie answered by saying,

"Nothing is wrong Jeff why?"

Jeff answered her by saying in a concerned voice,

"But Mother you have never worn your robe past eight o'clock in the morning. Mother I have someone here to see you."

Dottie took a hard look at Kamala and asked a surprising question;

"That isn't little. Kamala, it can't be?"

Kamala told Dottie anxiously,

"It sure is me, Dottie, you remembered me!"

Dottie said with assurance,

"Of course, I remembered you; how have you been, child?"

Jeff quickly said,

"Mother, Kamala needs your help. She needs information about what you might know of her Father."

30

Dottie asked Kamala with a long face about her,

"How is it that I might know your Father?"

Kamala took the letter out of her pocket and handed it over to Dottie. She looked it over and over and tried to read it. She recognized the hand writing and slowly said,

"That's my hand writing alright. I'm surprised you could even read that chicken scratch. Now child why is it so important that you need information about your Father? I haven't seen Jim in twenty years".

Kamala surprisingly said,

"You did know my Father! You see my Father happened to had a heart-attack and....." she stopped,

Dottie said with concern in her voice,

"Oh child, Jim didn't die, did he?"

Kamala just hung her head.

Dottie continued saying,

"Now child, this is a lot to process here."

Kamala asked her,

"Dottie do you by any chance have anything of my Father's that I can use for the funeral? I have so little to go on. I lived with my Father until the law came for me and that's when you got me. I would appreciate it ever so much Dottie."

Dottie said apologetically,

"Kamala, I'm so sorry you have lost your Father. Jim was a very kind man."

Dottie kept talking and added,

"I never had any idea that Jim was your Father or even had any children. He never made mention of any."

31

Kamala was very surprised to even hear that and Dottie asked,

"Why is it that your Father raised you for only seven years, what happened to your Mother?"

Kamala had a lump in her throat and started crying. Dottie said to Kamala,

"Now child don't cry, I'm sorry I asked you."

Kamala composed herself and told Dottie,

"When my Mother was pregnant with me she hadn't been married to my Father and she was sent to a home for unwed Mothers and my Father....He stole me away from there."

Dottie said,

"It's all coming together now. It must have been rough for you Kamala to find out all that about your Mother, I do apologize. Oh yes, you needed some information about your Father so you......can she just stop right then."

Kamala said to her,

"We can put my Father to rest. It's ok Dottie."

Dottie went to her bedroom and came out with papers Kamala's Father had given to her before he had left. Kamala took them and started reading what she had given to her. She anxiously said,

"Dottie, you.... didn't mention that my Father had been in the military."

Dottie mention to Kamala,

"I had no idea. I just took those papers from your Father before he left I had not read them. He only told me to save them, so naturally I did."

Kamala read on and found out why her Father had left Dottie and told her,

"My Father had to join the service or go to jail. He was ordered by the courts to pay child support for me."

Dottie said,

"That's how I was able to raise you Kamala, but after you were taken from me, the money stopped."

Kamala continued that conversation by saying,

"That's when I was taken to Camp Washington to those other people. Then the money was transferred to them. After that, I ended up in Milford close to where I am living now. At that time the money was transferred to there until I became the age of 18 and that's when I went on my own."

Dottie told Kamala,

"Kamala I had no idea what had happened to you. I'm sorry for all you've had to go through child."

Kamala found a birth certificate of her Father and numerous photos of him and her together and of her Father when he was a child and pictures of him and her Mother. Kamala asked Dottie,

"How can I repay you?"

Dottie answered Kamala very suddenly,

"Yes of course! You can marry my son!"

Kamala and Jeff just looked at one another and he told his Mother while moving his head back and forth,

"Now Mother!"

Kamala told Jeff,

"It's probably best that I will be moving on."

Jeff, Reassured Kamala by saying,

"You're not going alone because I'm, returning with you. I need to be getting back home and Kamala, you don't need to be riding the bus alone and that's that."

When the two got back to Milford they got off the bus and walked together to Kamala's home. That's......

<u>The Ghost Town story.</u>

CHAPTER NINE

Irish Coffee

W hen Kamala and Jeff went inside of her brick home all of sudden, she recalled it was the 17th day of March therefore she put on a pot of Irish Coffee. While it was brewing the aroma of Irish Whiskey swept across the kitchen. When Jeff sniffed the air, his nose detected what it was and he asked

Kamala respectfully,

"Is that Irish Coffee I smell?"

Kamala answered Jeff with an irritable voice,

"Yes! it is Jeff! What about it?"

Jeff dared not to ask anything else but Kamala asked him,

"Jeff have you ever had Irish Coffee?"

While Kamala was getting two coffee mugs and a stein out of her China Cabinet Jeff stayed quiet for a few minutes then he asked Kamala with a stern voice,

"What has happened to you Kamala? Have I said something to offend you?"

Kamala replied while setting the mugs and stein on the kitchen counter next to the coffee pot,

"Why no Jeff, why do you ask?"

Jeff answered slowly cautiously,

"Ieeeee was just wondering."

Kamala asked Jeff with a harsh voice,

"Wondering what Jeff?"

Jeff replied,

"You sound sarcastic when you speak now. What's all that about Kamala?"

While Kamala was filling the mugs and the stein with the Irish Coffee, she looked at Jeff with an apologetic face and said with kindness in her voice,

"I do apologize, Jeff, I just have a lot on my mind so let's just enjoy the moment."

Jeff helped Kamala by setting everything else on the kitchen table. In a short time, Kamala went to the refrigerator to get the can of whipping cream out, and when she turned around and faced

Jeff, he took the can from her and started to squirt the cream over top of the coffee but nothing came out; only a sound of air.

Kamala irritably jerked the can from Jeff's hands and bluntly said while shaking the can vigorously and clenching her teeth,

"Jeff! You've got to shake the can first!"

Jeff said nothing but looked at Kamala with an expression of empathy and took Kamala into his arms. Not too awful long after that the two ended up in the guest room together; there went the idea of enjoying.......

Irish Coffee.

CHAPTER TEN

She Felt Outraged

U pon awakening Kamala extended her arms out to stretch but when she tried to straighten out her legs she felt her distance was shortened by another body. All of sudden she recalled she had slept with Jeff. Kamala felt outraged when she realized she was in the guest room and remembered when she slept there alone and why. She yelled out in a belligerent voice,

"Jeff, how could you!" She startled Jeff awake and he almost jumped up out of bed but then recalled he had nothing on and stayed under the covers and said loudly,

"How could I what Kamala?"

After a few seconds, Kamala recalled that hadn't been just Jeff's decision, it was hers too, and said,

"I'm sorry Jeff, I just recalled when I slept here alone and why I did and remembered what I have to do today."

Kamala wrapped the top sheet around her and left the room to take a shower. Jeff got dressed and went to the kitchen and threw out the stale Irish Coffee and put a regular pot of coffee. While it was brewing he exchanged rooms with Kamala and took a shower.

Kamala got dressed and went to the kitchen to make breakfast for them. When she finished she called to Jeff and said anxiously?

"Jeff, I hope you're hungry because I made plenty for the both of us!?"

After they ate and cleaned up the kitchen Kamala picked up the pile of papers that Dottie had given her and started Looking through them and was wondering if she could afford the cost of her Father's funeral. She came across some papers that stated her Father would be buried at the Arlington Military Cemetery in Dayton, Ohio. Kamala was somewhat relieved after that and started making phone calls to make arrangements for her Father's layout and services. She was told not to worry about all of the details because they would handle all the preparations and reassured Kamala with a kind and caring voice, saying,

"Young lady all you have to do is to Drop off your Father's military DD214 form and anything else that pertains to him that you think might be helpful to complete arrangements."

Kamala started to leave the house and Jeff asked her,

"Kamala, where are you heading off to young lady?"

Kamala told Jeff in an apologetic voice,

"I'm sorry Jeff, I'd forgotten all about you. I don't know where my head is, I'm not thinking right."

Jeff told Kamala,

"I'm here to help you all the way so let's go get that bus together because you don't need to be taking it by yourself."

Kamala told Jeff nicely,

"Thanks, Jeff, I need all the help I can get, that's why I called you in the first place. Thanks again, Jeff."

When Kamala and Jeff got to their destination they left the bus near the Arlington Cemetery they walked across to the building they had been directed to and talked to the person that was in charge. They handed him her Father's DD 214 form and photos that Dottie had given Kamala.

After a few hours, all the arrangements had been made. When the two left the building, Kamala felt emotional and started sobbing. Jeff took her in his arms to comfort her and told her with an empathetic voice,

"Now Kamala chin up, things will be ok. I'm with you all the way, all through everything, so you just remember that young lady, ok?"

Kamala couldn't help herself from sobbing the entire way back to her home and when they went inside Kamala felt extremely ashamed and apologized to Jeff saying,

"I'm very sorry for the way I have behaved today Jeff."

Jeff replied,

"Nonsense, don't you worry yourself about that."

Jeff asked Kamala with a concerned voice,

"Kamala why don't you take a nap. It's been a long afternoon for you and I'll cook dinner if it that's ok with you?"

Kamala didn't think twice about the idea of taking a nap and went to her bedroom and cried herself to sleep while Jeff was cooking dinner. When Jeff finished he went to the bedroom to see if Kamala was awake but she wasn't so Jeff left the room and went back to the kitchen and ate his dinner alone.

After he was finished he started to clean up then heard Kamala coming down the hallway. She was sobbing and he welcomed her with his open arms to comfort her. She so appreciated his kindness. Kamala wasn't feeling outraged anymore and felt safe in Jeff's arms.

CHAPTER ELEVEN

With Integrity

After a few days went by Kamala and Jeff got dressed suitable for her Father's funeral then caught a bus to Dayton, OH. When the bus arrived at their destination Kamala saw in the near distance a green canopy sheltering a freshly dug gravesite. She just knew it was for her Father. It didn't take long before tears started rolling down her checks then she placed her hands over her face then she started tapping it with her fingers then cried out,

"No Daddy! No Daddy! You can't leave me now. I just found you, Daddy!"

When Kamala pulled herself together Jeff suggested,

"Kamala, it's best that we get to the chapel before anyone else does, don't you think?"

When they entered the chapel, Kamala cast her eyes upon pictures of her Father that had been projected onto a screen and cried out, while putting her hands across her face,

"I'm done! I'm done!"

Jeff could feel her pain and held her in his arms to comfort her. He took Kamala to another room and helped her to a seat and seated himself. While they were holding hands, she longed for his strength from the beginning to the end of the services in the chapel.

Since it was a military Funeral the ceremony at the gravesite was overpowering for Kamala. With the twenty-one-gun salute and the taps being played in the near distance, the sound traveled through the air. Then there was another bugle being played at a farther distance that echoed it. The sympathy and sincerity of it all was overwhelming. Kamala accepted the tightly rolled up American Flag in the honor of her Father......

<u>With Integrity.</u>

CHAPTER TWELVE

If You Could Go Anywhere, Where Would It Be?

Before leaving the grounds Kamala hovered over her Father's coffin and kissed it and told her Father sadly,

"Good Bye Daddy, I'll see you in heaven."

Not too long after that, the minister handed Kamala a large yellow envelope with her Father's pictures and the important papers that he had needed for the services. Kamala and Jeff then took the bus back to her home.

When they reached their destination, the two went inside.

Kamala made a special place for the American Flag and put the envelope on her desk. They were both tuckered out so they took a nap.

Upon awakening the two felt hungry so Kamala went to the kitchen to cook but nothing sounded good to her so she suggested to Jeff,

"Jeff, would pizza be ok for dinner?"

Jeff was fine with that suggestion so Kamala picked up the telephone and ordered one to be delivered. After they ate there wasn't much to clean up but the aroma of pepperoni still lingered in the air.

Kamala went to her desk to get that yellow envelope that had been handed back to her. A picture of her Father and Jeff's Mother fell out. When she picked it up then she stared at her Father's face for the longest time. She noticed that Jeff and he had some similar features. She recognized their noses were a perfect match. It couldn't be though because he had lived with his Father; or did he? Kamala started thinking that her father might possibly be Jeff's Father too.

Kamala took a second look at the picture and noticed that her Father and Jeff had the same chin but Jeff had his Mother's eyes. Kamala started thinking hard and she asked herself out loud,

"I don't want to go there but was Dottie seeing my Father at the same time she was with the man that's supposed to be Jeff's Father?"

She continued those thoughts with,

"Na, it couldn't be...or could it?"

While things were still fresh in her mind about her Father's services she started typing out that story. She would type a while and stop and take another glance at the photo then lay it down and kept typing, trying not to think about what she was seeing.

Just about that time, Jeff was feeling left out of Kamala's life. He was about to tell her that he was going somewhere else but then he had no idea where he would go. He went to Kamala and asked her,

"If You Could Go Anywhere, Where Would It Be?"

CHAPTER THIRTEEN

How Much Time Do We Have?

K amala didn't have an answer for Jeff. She just stared at him while studying his facial features and comparing his nose and chin to her Father's, Jeff asked Kamala,

"What are you doing?"

Kamala prolonged answering Jeff for a few minutes and held the photo up to his face. Jeff was getting antsy and asked Kamala with concern,

"What are you doing, Kamala?"

Jeff took the photo out of Kamala's hand and stared at it and asked Kamala,

"Is there something in this picture that I need to know about, Kamala? If there is, please let me know what you see that I don't?"

Kamala asked Jeff,

"How much time do we have?"

Jeff replied,

"Time to do what, Kamala?"

Kamala, with mind boggled thoughts, said to Jeff,

"Look at the picture and you tell me what you see?"

Jeff took the photo and examined it thoroughly and held it up to his face while looking into the mirror and asked Kamala,

"Ok Kamala, I give up, what is that you see here?"

44

Kamala replied,

"Jeff you and my Father has the same nose and chin!"

Jeff quickly said,

"Of course, we do Kamala!"

Kamala was surprised at Jeff's response and said anxiously,

"I knew it!"

Jeff asked her,

"You knew what Kamala?"

She answered Jeff by asking,

"By any chance could my Father be yours too Jeff?"

Jeff started laughing and told Kamala,

"No Kamala, your Father was my Uncle!"

Kamala looked at Jeff in doubt and asked him,

"How could that be, because your last name is Johnson and my Father's last name is Jackson?"

and he replied,

"Well, Kamala it's like this, when my Mother gave birth to me she wasn't married at the time and her maiden name is Johnson."

Jeff added to that before Kamala could say anything,

"My Mother and Father married after I was born. She kept her maiden name along with her married name, but after my parents divorced she didn't use her married name again."

Kamala asked Jeff,

"What you're telling me is that your Father didn't adopt you, am I right Jeff?"

Jeff answered her with assurance,

45

"That's the way it was. You answered your own question, Kamala."

She told Jeff in a surprised voice,

"I had no idea that my Father had a brother."

Then Kamala and Jeff said at the same time,

"Oh my gosh, that makes us cousins!"

Kamala was freakish about that idea and said,

"Do you mean you knew my Father was your Uncle and we slept together and you said nothing? How could you Jeff!?"

Jeff told Kamala,

"I'm sorry Kamala, I didn't know that until today."

Jeff continued with,

"Not just that Kamala, with your name being Waits, how could I have known that?"

Kamala was still freakish about the whole situation of her and Jeff and ask him,

"What about Dottie? She must have known we were cousins and she still had enough nerve to tell me to marry her son. I can't believe that she would even suggest that. There must have been some reason she would even hint for us to marry!?"

Jeff told Kamala with a respective answer,

"Kamala, remember my Mother told you she didn't know that your Father was Jim or even had any children and she didn't know your Father was a brother to my Father. But I did read it in a letter that my Father had received from yours many years ago. That's when I learned that your Father was my Father's brother."

Jeff continued,

"Now what do we do now Kamala?"

46

She replied by saying with anger in her voice,

"You're asking me, what to do now? You must be kidding Jeff!"

Jeff just leave before I throw something!

Jeff asked her,

"Kamala, do you really mean that? Can't we at least be kissing cousins?"

Kamala told Jeff in a stern voice,

"It can't work Jeff, because kissing cousins don't sleep together, so please leave, just go Jeff!"

Jeff told Kamala in a serious voice,

"But Kamala, I have fallen in love with you...in capital letters. Do I have to leave you now? Are you sure you want me to go just like that?"

Kamala said to Jeff in a perturbed voice,

"Stop right there Jeff, don't you hear me? Just leave!"

Jeff wasn't going anywhere. Instead, he picked up Kamala and carried her to her bedroom with Kamala fighting all the way and telling him while clenching her teeth and hitting him with her fists.

"Put me down, Jeff! Put me down! I mean it, Jeff!"

Before Kamala could say another word, Jeff lowered Kamala to the bed and started to leave the room. Kamala asked Jeff,

"What are you doing Jeff?"

Jeff said seriously,

"Leaving!"

Kamala asks him,

"Why?"

Jeff couldn't believe what Kamala asked him, then said,

"You told me to leave, so that's what I am doing!"

Kamala asked Jeff,

"Seriously Jeff?"

Jeff answered Kamala with a question,

"You want me, don't you?"

Kamala started stripping off her clothes and said,

"What do you think?"

Jeff asked Kamala,

"What about us being cousins and all?"

Kamala motioned for Jeff to come to her. Jeff didn't think twice about that proposal. Time was no factor to this situation. Neither one asked.

How Much Time Do We Have?

CHAPTER FOURTEEN

We Are Not Ourselves When We Are Upset

After a few days had passed and Kamala glanced at the calendar she recalled she had almost missed out on one of the most important days of her life. Kamala was to be honored for the 1200 fairytales she had written over the past twelve years. It dawned on her that she needed to shop for the most beautiful dress she had ever worn. Her hair looked unkept and there-fore she needed to have her hair cut and styled. She noticed it was almost noon, so she scheduled her hair appointment before going shopping.

When Kamala started to walk out the door her telephone rang. She recognized it was Dottie when she picked up the receiver Dottie's voice sounded so panicked and Kamala yelled for Jeff to come to the telephone. When he didn't come right away she remembered he had left earlier that morning. Kamala just knew it wasn't going to be a good day. She asked Dottie with an anxious voice,

"What is it, Dottie? What's going on?"

Dottie replied with a sense of urgency in her voice,

"Kamala, I have to see you...!"

Kamala remembered what Dottie had said to her as a child before going out to play,

"Be the friend you would want to have."

Kamala loved Dottie and yearned to be the friend she herself would want to have and after all, she was sleeping with Dottie's son. She reassured Dottie,

"Dottie I'll be there as quickly as I can."

Kamala caught the first bus to Camp Washington and when she got to Dottie's house she saw Dottie waiting outside for her and saying,

"Hurry Kamala! Hurry please!"

Kamala didn't see anything wrong at first then she started feeling angry. She just couldn't have this day ruined over anything, but then she remembered someone telling her,

"We are not ourselves when we are upset."

Kamala told herself,

"Stay calm Kamala! Stay calm!"

Kamala went over to Dottie and asked her.

"What is it, Dottie? What's wrong?"

Dottie took Kamala inside her home anxiously, then told her while twisting her hands,

"Sit child."

Kamala then asked her,

"What's going on Dottie?"

Dottie looked at Kamala with concern, then... told her,

"You can't marry my son, I mean your...."

she stopped. Kamala just stared at Dottie and questioned her,

"He's my what......?"

she stopped, Dottie told Kamala slowly,

"Beeeeecause he's your brother!"

Kamala stood up then asked Dottie with a sense of urgency in her voice and trying to stay calm,

"How could that be Dottie? How Dottie? You've got to tell me!"

Kamala finished, by saying,

"He can't be, because he's your son. He told me that he had lived with his..."

Kamala stopped then Dottie told Kamala with a serious voice,

"Yes, Jeff is my son but his Father is your......."

she stopped then Kamala just looked at her with uncertainty and said,

"My Father is Jeff's Father!? That can't be because he said he lived with his Father."

Dottie told Kamala in an apologetic voice,

"I'm sorry Kamala, I had to tell you before...."

she stopped and Kamala asked Dottie in a very serious voice,

"Why did you tell me to marry your son when you knew he was my brother? How could you Dottie?"

Dottie replied,

"Well Kamala I haven't been my usual self lately and when I told you to marry my son, I wasn't serious about all of that; but Jeff told me that you and he were having......"

she stopped, Kamala finished her sentence by saying,

"Having sex!"

Kamala continued saying,

"Are you sure that my Father is Jeff's Father?"

Dottie didn't hesitate and said,

"I'm sure Kamala because Jim is the one that I had slept with when I had gotten pregnant with Jeff."

Kamala asked Dottie in a very serious voice,

"What about the man that was supposed to have been Jeff's Father?"

Dottie explained by saying,

"I was with him a few weeks after Jim. That's why he thought he was Jeff's Father. Nothing was said at that time until I told him differently."

"That's why John and I ended up in a divorce. But he hadn't told Jeff anything because he didn't want to hurt Jeff. I didn't know that John was Jim's brother until my son Jeff showed me the letter Jim had written to his brother John while he was in the military."

Kamala felt as if she had the wind knocked out of her. She just stared at the ceiling with her eyes wide open and remained silent for the longest time. Dottie asked Kamala in a frantic voice,

"Are you ok child? Can I get you something?"

Kamala asked Dottie anxiously,

"Does Jeff know that my Father was his Father also Dottie?"

Dottie started twisting her hands again and said,

"I don't think so!"

Kamala asked Dottie in a serious tone,

"Don't you think you should tell Jeff?"

Jeff walked in and asked,

"Tell me what Kamala?"

Kamala looked over at Dottie and said,

"Go ahead Dottie, tell him or I will!"

Dottie mustered up enough courage and said nervously,

"There's something I've got to tell you son."

Jeff answered quickly,

"What's that Mother?"

Dottie told Jeff slowly,

"Jeff, Johns not.... your Father!"

Surprisingly, Jeff said,

"I knew he wasn't because he had told me but what I didn't know was that Jim was my Father until you told me just now; Mother, how long were you going to keep that a secret, how could you!" Dottie told Jeff with an apologetic voice,

"I'm sorry Jeff, I should have told you long before this, especially knowing about you and Kamala."

Jeff started sobbing hard. Kamala went over to him to comfort him.

Jeff asked his Mother after he had composed himself,

"Do you mean I have buried my Father just a few days ago and nothing was said to that fact?"

Jeff glared at Kamala and asked her,

"What about us now, what happens now Kamala to us; this whole thing stinks?"

Kamala started thinking about what she had been doing before she went to Dottie's and said,

"I know this sounds tacky after all that, that just happened this afternoon but I have a date with the red carpet. I should be leaving; Jeff can I count on you being there?"

Jeff answered unexpectedly,

"Of course, I will Kamala, why wouldn't I?"

Kamala and Jeff picked up their wraps and left to catch the bus to Milford. When they got to Kamala's home, Kamala looked at Jeff as if to say,

"I'm sorry about all of this. I could have gone home myself but I'm more than happy to have my brother right beside me all the way. I do need to get changed now before I'm late!"

Kamala wore her wig until she got to the ceremony and one of her pretties dresses she had hanging in her closet. She went out to the living room where Jeff was waiting and remembered she needed to cancel her hair appointment; done, Jeff looked at Kamala anxiously saying,

"I'm sorry Kamala; I mean sis. Let's go get them, tiger!"

That's the story about.....

We Are Not Ourselves, When We Are Upset.

CHAPTER FIFTEEN

A Bouquet Of Field Flowers

When Kamala and Jeff walked to the Milford Shopping Center where the ceremonial dinner was being held for. Kamala they took their usual path and when they stepped inside Kamala was overwhelmed by the crowd and started feeling nervous; she put her face in her hands and started tapping her face and Jeff noticed and told her,

"Kamala...I mean sis, let's get you to the holding room where you're supposed to be, tiger!"

After Jeff got Kamala to the room he left her and went to the auditorium where the audience was waiting impatiently and took a seat in the first row so he could have the perfect view.

When the speaker walked up on stage he took hold of the microphone and announced Kamala's name for recognized fame. The crowd stood up and applauded vigorously. When she took that first step into the isle way, instantly the spotlight beamed on her and every step she was taking. The crowd gave her a five-minute standing ovation. As she walked down the red-carpet that was laid out for her, her long reddish-brown hair was blowing gently around her face and down passed her waist.

When Kamala took the first steps onto the stage, her green eyes sparkled like glass. When she smiled, her high-check bones heightened even more. She was beautiful!

Kamala's Orchid Dress created a flattering fit with a flirty asymmetrical hem line that made her look smashing. Jeff's eyes were wide-open. He was amazed and his eyes filled with tearful awe. Jeff stood up applauding and said anxiously and loudly,

"Boy she looks ravishing, doesn't she!"

The crowd replied by saying, with a loud sound, that echoed everywhere

"She sure does!"

When the speaker placed a sparkling jeweled crown on her head in honor of her victory she was given a plaque that read,

Congratulations Kamala Rae Waits, for all the hard work and effort you have put forth in writing over 1200 fairytales in the past twelve years of your life. The years of 1970-1982.

As the speaker was reading aloud what was written on Kamala's plaque she modestly put her hands across her face and started tapping her fingers, crying out with excitement, Then Jeff came up on the stage and hugged Kamala and handed her.......

A Bouquet Of Field Flowers.

CHAPTER SIXTEEN

The Author's Forthcoming Book

When the banquet was over Kamala and Jeff were escorted to Kamala's home in a gold colored limousine as a gesture of honor.

Before Kamala and Jeff went inside, the driver asked Kamala,

"So, what's The Author's Forthcoming Book?"

Kamala answered by saying with much joy,

"A Baby Book!"

Jeff looked at Kamala with such surprise and asked her,

"Did I hear you right Kamala?"

Kamala replied by asking him with a big smile across her face,

"You heard me right Jeff, why?"

Jeff said with flattering words,

"You fox you!"

Kamala asked Jeff in a confused voice,

"What about us being cousins? I mean brother and sister; heck I don't know what I mean, Jeff! All of this is making me crazy!"

Jeff replied,

"Who cares? We're going to have a baby!"

Kamala asked Jeff in a serious voice,

"Now where do we stand? I mean, where do I stand with you?"

Jeff kneeled down and asked Kamala,

"Girl, will you be my bride?"

Kamala replied with a wry expression,

"No, I won't marry you, Jeff! You know we can't marry one another, but what I do know is that I need you by my side all through this. You will, won't you?"

Jeff replied,

"Boy, this is all weird, Kamala. But as to your question; of course, I will! You should know that. Don't you?"

Kamala told Jeff with a serious answer,

"Yes, of course, I know that, Jeff!"

Kamala took hold of Jeff and said,

"Kiss me, you big Gluck!"

Jeff replied by saying,

"What about......"

he stopped and

Kamala said,

"It's too late for that Jeff, kiss me!"

What Kamala and Jeff didn't know was that the driver of the limousine told one person that Kamala's forthcoming book was to be a baby book and when the media got hold of that information, the word got around pretty fast; And when Dottie heard,

she called Jeff and asked him,

"Is that true what I heard, that Kamala is going to have a baby?"

Jeff replied,

"Who told you, I just found that out myself Mother! How did you know?"

Dottie replied with a serious voice,

"Jeff, the whole world knows!"

Jeff almost dropped his telephone but looked at Kamala with a puzzled expression. Kamala looked back at him questionably,

"What is it Jeff, what's going on?"

Jeff told Kamala,

"We'll talk later ok?"

She looked at Jeff and she nodded her head yes and said,

"Ok."

Jeff told his Mother he would get back with her later and hung up. Now Jeff told Kamala what his Mother had said to him and she replied,

"It's not Dottie's...it's ours and we'll deal with it our way."

Jeff asked Kamala with a serious tone,

"Who told the world about our baby?"

Kamala said,

"Remember Jeff, the driver of the limousine asked me, what my forthcoming book was going to be?"

Jeff replied,

"Oh well, that's the media for you alright; once they get hold of some news it's public announcement but that's ok with me. How about you Kamala?"

Kamala answered,

" Let's celebrate, let the whole world know, I don't care.

Jeff asked Kamala,

"What about my Mother, she could cause a big scandal for us?"

Kamala replied with a joyful tone,

"We could tell the world what she had done to you by not telling you who your Father was. Let's celebrate and have our baby and happy life together. What do you say, Jeff?"

Jeff asked Kamala,

"How about that kiss?"

Kamala said quickly,

"Absolutely!"

Now the world knows about

The Author's Forthcoming Book.

CHAPTER SEVENTEEN

Disrespectful, Wicked, Evil-Minded People

Day after day Kamala received anonymous phone calls asking her frightful questions,

"Who's going to raise your illegitimate child, Kamala?"

"Kamala, is your baby going to know who it's father is?"

"Kamala is your baby going to know who it's Mother is?"

"Kamala, are you going to give your baby away?"

Kamala told every one of them while gritting her teeth,

"You're nothing but disrespectful, wicked, evil-mined people, how dare you pass judgment on me!"

If that wasn't enough...every morning Kamala had nausea, vomiting, dizziness sometimes accompanied by headaches, and besides all of this other craziness, she was cranky, and irritable too.

Kamala got tired of feeling ill, so she decided to make appointment with her Gynecologist. When it was time for her appointment, she took the usual route to the bus but all of a sudden, she felt dizzy and fell to the ground. Someone had seen her and dialed 911 shortly before that. She found herself in an emergency room. She informed the doctors that she was pregnant. After he examined her he had sad news to tell her. He said with much concern,

"I'm sorry young lady, but...."

he stopped and Kamala asked him in an anxious voice,

"But what doctor?"

He tried to finish his statement by saying,

"You have lost......."

he stopped and Kamala asked him very seriously,

"Have I lost my.........."

Jeff stepped into the room and overheard Kamala and asked her,

"You have lost what, Kamala?"

Kamala started crying when the doctor told her,

"You have lost your baby, young lady, I'm sorry to say!"

Kamala started sobbing and between sniffles, she cried out!

"Jeff, I have.... lost our baby!"

Jeff took Kamala in his arms to comfort her. He had no words to say now, he felt her pain and just cried with her. What a sad moment for the two.

CHAPTER EIGHTEEN

I'm Missing A Book

After Kamala had been home from the hospital for about a week, all of sudden she remembered; her, ideas of writing for the baby book she had purchased earlier flashed through her mind. She rummaged through all 1200 fairytale books that she had written, lining the shelves of the guestroom. She couldn't find it. She yelled for Jeff. When Jeff entered the room, he asked her with concern,

"What's going on Kamala?"

She looked at him with a puzzled face, and told Jeff in a perturbed voice,

"I'm missing a book!"

Jeff asked her,

"What book is that Kamala?"

Kamala replied,

"A baby book!"

Jeff was troubled about that. He asked,

"What baby book, Kamala?"

She was getting more upset and responded with a much louder voice,

"You remember Jeff, the one I was going to write in, about our baby!"

Jeff felt awkward about the idea and asked her,

"Kamala, how can you write about a miscarriage, we don't have any idea if our baby was a boy or girl!"

Kamala told Jeff with much anxiety,

"It's the experience I'll never forget. It's the experience I want to share with the world!"

Jeff asked Kamala,

"What about the disrespectful, wicked, evil-minded people?"

Kamala replied,

"Writing has always played a significant role in my life but this story will be about the loss of life, our baby, our child!"

Jeff asked Kamala seriously,

"What will you name the baby?"

Kamala replied,

"Well Jeff, it could have been both, a boy and a girl, I'm giving the world both. The boy's name will be Kevin and the girl's name will be Leha. What do you think?"

Finally, Jeff found the baby book that Kamala had been looking for and said,

"Here's your baby book Kamala. I found it on your desk; have fun writing but be truthful about everything. I mean be honest about it all, ok Kamala?"

Kamala replied in a reassuring voice,

"Nothing but the truth Jeff! Nothing but the truth..."

That's the story about.........

I'm Missing A Book.

CHAPTER NINETEEN

Box Lunch

Kamala was having a combination of happiness and unhappiness this day. No matter what she typed for her forthcoming book, nothing was making any sense to her when she would read what she had written all morning long. Kamala had crumbled up and thrown away more paper than ever before while writing. She would laugh very little and cried out a lot.

Kamala decided to turn to her cedar chest where she had stored receiving blankets, bibs, tee-shirts, bottles, diapers, baby outfits for boys and girls including baby toys and bottoms she had purchased. She would cuddle the baby items up to her face and cried out and laughed very little.

Jeff noticed by the pencil marks on the calendar that it was May the 1st. He had no idea what the significance was. Jeff specially made some pan-fried chicken and added side-dishes, then he made an Italian Creme Cheese Cake. After he was done, he put everything in a box and added some sodas. Then Jeff went to Kamala and asked her,

"Kamala, what's the reason the calendar is marked for today? Is it some special day?"

Kamala replied by asking Jeff,

"Well, what day is it, Jeff?"

Jeff said,

"May the first, why?"

Kamala had forgotten it was her birthday. She told Jeff with an anxious voice,

"Jeff, it's my birthday!"

Jeff asked Kamala,

"How about you and I go to the park for a picnic; how about it, Kamala?"

Kamala replied,

"Well, I'll need to cook up something to take and make a cake. Sounds fun Jeff, give me a few minutes, and I'll be ready."

Jeff told Kamala with a joyful voice,

"Kamala, I'm way ahead of you!"

Kamala asked him,

"How's that?"

Jeff answered,

"I fixed us a box lunch Kamala and it's waiting in the kitchen for us, let's go ok?"

Kamala didn't think twice and put her long reddish brown-hair up in a ponytail and put on her ball cap and told Jeff,

"Ok, let's go, Jeff, I'm ready!"

Kamala and Jeff walked to the nearest park ate and played on the monkey bars and the merry-go-round. Kamala and Jeff were laughing and having all kinds of fun. Jeff told Kamala,

"Boy, it's good to hear you laughing and having fun Kamala!!" Before Jeff cut the cake, he sang, "Happy Birthday" to Kamala. Kamala told Jeff,

"Now we need to dance around the maypole!"

Jeff asked her,

"Do what Kamala?"

She told him,

"It's traditional to dance around the maypole on the first day of May and to crown a May queen with flowers..."

So, they took some clover flowers and made a garland wreath, Jeff placed it on Kamala's head and the two danced around the pole that was cemented in the ground for that purpose and had a fantastically fun day and returned home that evening.

Jeff asked Kamala,

"How is your forthcoming book?"

Kamala had no answer to that question but what she did tell Jeff was,

"Thanks, Jeff, for all you have done for me so we could have a happy and fun day, especially for that........."

Box Lunch.

CHAPTER TWENTY

For What Reason

It was five o'clock in the morning and someone was rapping on the kitchen door. By the time Kamala had gotten up and walked down the hall the rapping stopped. She started to go back to bed but the rapping started all over again. This time it was the Livingroom door. By the time she got there to answer it no one was there. Kamala looked all around but saw nothing.

Before she went back to bed, she peeked out front at her mail box attached to the brick wall; she noticed the box door was open and she knew she always closed it after getting her mail. Kamala took a look. Inside the box was a white envelope. Taking it out, it felt kind of heavy. This was odd because it was over the amount of weight for this size of an envelope...

Kamala sat down on her stoop and before she opened the envelope, she noticed that it didn't have an address to who it was being sent to, or even a return address. When Kamala opened the envelope, she was amazed to see so much money.

Kamala went inside to count the money. When she was walking down the hallway to the kitchen Jeff came out of the guest room. He saw Kamala and was wondering why she was up so early. He asked,

"Kamala, what's going on? Why are you up at such an hour?"

Kamala looked at Jeff with a confused look and replied while holding the envelope open and facing Jeff,

"Look, Jeff!"

Jeff took a hard look at what she had and answered with a question,

"Where did you get all of that?"

Kamala replied,

"It was in the mail box."

Jeff and Kamala sat down at the kitchen table and turned the light on above then Kamala laid the money on the table. The two had a puzzled look on their faces when they counted it. There was ten-thousand-dollar bills and a note that read,

"Use it as you wish."

Jeff asked,

"Who would have done such a thing and......."

For What Reason?

CHAPTER TWENTY-ONE

The 73-Year-old Man

Kamala replied,

"They're awfully generous, whoever they are!"

And Kamala heard some-body outside. It sounded as if they were rummaging through her trash cans. She placed her hands across her face and started tapping her face again with her fingers and when Jeff saw her doing so he knew something had to be wrong. He asked her in a concerned voice...,

"What's wrong Kamala?"

Kamala was speechless. All she could do was stare at the window. Jeff got up and looked out and saw a grey-haired old man going. Through the trash cans and went to the door and asked him,

"What are you looking for old-man?"

The old-man replied with an anxious voice,

"Money!"

Jeff asked him,

"How much money?"

The old-man replied,

"Ten thousand smackers!"

Jeff replied with a question,

"How much money did you say?"

The old-man answered him,

"Ten thousand smackers, I told you!"

Jeff asked,

"What are you doing with that kind of money?"

The old-man replied,

"It was my life savings. I took it out of the bank to pay for my funeral expenses."

Jeff asked the old-man,

"What gives you the idea it's around here?"

The old-man replied,

"I was waiting for a bus, going to Cincinnati to see someone and then I was going to the Baltimore Pike Cemetery to pay my dues. I bent over, I dropped the money out of my pocket someone picked it up and ran with it. I followed him here but when I couldn't find him, I decided to look in the trash can just in case he might have put it there to hide it."

Jeff asked the old man,

"Why would they hide it in the trash can?"

The seventy some year-old man replied,

"After he realized what it was he probably became scared and didn't want anyone to find out what he had and stashed it somewhere."

Jeff looked over at Kamala in question and asked,

"What should we do?"

Kamala asked the man,

"If we found the money, how much would we get as a reward?"

Jeff said to her,

"Kamala, that was the man's life savings!"

Kamala replied anxiously,

"It doesn't hurt to ask, does it?"

Jeff told Kamala,

"Give....Give the old man his money!"

She did and felt good about it. The old man asked her,

"Where did you find it?"

Kamala told him and the old man started to offer them a reward....
but...

They told him to keep it, it was his money; and so, he did and
went on.

CHAPTER TWENTY-TWO

Good Behavior

Kamala was wondering who was that seventy some year-old grey haired man who claimed that the ten thousand smackers was his and who was he going to see in Cincinnati. To Kamala, he looked kind of familiar it was like she had seen his face somewhere.

She thought for a few minutes then she went to her old desk and picked up the large yellow envelope that Dottie had given to her that once belonged to her Father.

Kamala started looking through the pictures. She found one of her, her Mother and Father along with a man that looked identical to that very same man she had seen but much younger in years. Kamala got dressed for the day and went for a walk toward the diner where she and her Father had gone too. She carried the photo with her.

When Kamala went inside she showed the picture around and asked everyone while pointing to the stranger in the picture,

"Have you seen this man?"

No one seemed to recognize the man but one waitress told Kamala,

"I just waited on him a few minutes ago."

Kamala asked the waitress with an anxious voice,

"Do you know where he went?"

She replied,

"I'm not really sure but he was awfully generous!"

Kamala asked her,

"What do you mean?"

She replied,

"He tipped me a large bill and told me to keep it and went on his way."

Kamala asked with an anxious, tone,

"May I ask you how much?"

She replied suspiciously,

"Why must you know?"

Kamala told her the story about the stranger and him claiming the lot of money was his and asked the waitress,

"Are you sure you don't know where he went?"

She replied while looking at the newspaper and pointing to a photo,

"That's him! Oh my gosh, he's a fugitive!"

Kamala picked up the newspaper and compared his face with the photo she had and asked herself,

"I wonder why he is in this picture along with my parents?"

The answer was furnished when Kamala looked at the back of the photo; it read,

Jim Jackson, Marie Waits, and baby Kamala Rae Waits and Kamala's Grandpa Jerry Jackson.

Kamala started thinking,

"My Grandpa, a fugitive?!"

She read the newspaper column about the prisoner who was on the run for stealing 10 thousand dollars from a High Stakes Poker Game and let out on good behavior after serving 30 years for killing a young lady by the name of Marie Waits. She thought for a few minutes and told herself,

"Hummmm, I can't believe it, my own Grandpa was a killer, he killed my......!"

Kamala stopped and placed her hands across her face started tapping it with her fingers, the very same habit she picked up from her Father. Kamala sat down on the very same bench that her and her Father sat on when she had questions to ask him. Kamala was confused on what to do about this situation. She started thinking hard,

"Why didn't my Father tell me who killed my Mother!?"

"My own Grandpa Jackson is a killer, a thief plus he's wanted by the law." Kamala was terrified for her Grandpa. Kamala came upon another stumbling-block in her life. Kamala felt nothing she was confused and just sat there on the bench looking straight ahead. Her Grandpa Jackson was out on,

<u>Good Behavior.</u>

CHAPTER TWENTY-THREE

An Old Tub Of Clothing For The Homeless

After a few hours Kamala felt weary, tired and cold she had no idea why she was setting on the bench but she knew that she needed to find something to cover up with. Kamala started out walking down the sidewalk after a few minutes, she came across an old tub of clothing for the homeless. Before she knew it, she was rummaging through it looking for something to cover up with, she came across an old blanket that was kind of torn that was ok with Kamala, because she needed it.

Kamala threw the blanket over her shoulders then started walking again down the sidewalk, she had no idea where she was, she came upon the same bench she just left and laid down, and went to sleep. She sleeps until day break. Upon waking she was wondering what she was doing before this. Kamala was put into a state of uncertainty. She didn't know what had happened to her. Why was she sleeping on the bench? She wondered for what reason why was it so important to her to be where she was.

Kamala felt scared, lonely and hungry. Kamala reached with her hands in her pockets for money but what she pulled out instead was a photo and a newspaper. It dawned on her after she reread what was in the newspaper column about her Grandpa a thought came to her,

"Oh! Yell! I was on a mission looking for that seventy some year-old grey-haired man. The very same old man that was rummaging through my trash cans for money!"

Kamala started thinking harder,

"Oh! Yes, my Grandpa Jackson, he's the one the law is looking for because he had stolen a wad of money. Oh! No! I don't want to go there......" she stopped

because she didn't want to believe that her Grandpa was the one who killed her Mother. The thoughts were haughty her. It was like her brain was full of too much information to think about. Kamala started feeling dizzy so she sat down on the bench she put her hands across her face, started tapping it with her fingers. She heard someone scuffing their feet she pecked through her fingers and saw that grey-haired old man being handed cuffed by the police she said with a loud voice,

"Stop it!"

When Jeff heard Kamala's voice as he was coming around the corner, he felt relieved because he was out all night looking for her, he asked anxiously,

"What's going on Kamala?"

Kamala looked at Jeff with a questionable face, it was like she didn't know who he was. Her thinking was on her Grandpa being handed cuffed and anxiously said while pointing at him and the police officer,

"That's my Grandpa, stop them they're trying to arrest him!"

Jeff asked anxiously,

"Who is he, Kamala?"

Kamala yelled out while pointing at him again,

"He's my Grandpa stop them!"

Jeff asked,

"He's your Grandpa, are you sure?"

Kamala was getting frustrated and said loudly,

"Of course, I'm sure!"

Kamala showed Jeff the newspaper and photo, he reread what she did and looked at the picture in the paper and compared it with the photo of him and looked at the back of it and saw that the grey-haired old man was her grandpa. Kamala said anxiously,

"Stop! Them now! Jeff! They're taking my Grandpa Jackson away!"

Jeff felt relieved that Kamala knew who he was but he asked the police officer,

"What did the old man do officer?"

He answered him,

"He stole a large amount of money, why?"

Then the policeman put the old man in the back of his cruiser and he got in and drove off. Kamala started weeping and yelling at Jeff,

"Jeff! You got to do something!"

Jeff replied,

"What Kamala can I do?"

Kamala replied with a much louder tone,

"You! Got to stop the police from hurting my Grandpa!!"

Jeff said,

"It doesn't look good Kamala for your Grandpa."

Kamala looked at Jeff with an evil eye and said,

"My Grandpa didn't........"

She paused. Jeff asked her,

"Your Grandpa didn't do what Kamala?"

Kamala replied seriously,

"Kill my Mother!"

And started weeping much louder, Jeff asked her,

"How do you know that Kamala, and what does that have to do with what he has been arrested for now, he is the one that claimed that money was his, I guess we'll need to catch a bus to the Clermont County Jail and find out what's going on."

Kamala replied loudly,

"Because my Father would have told me that if it was true, and he told us that was his life savings."

Jeff asked,

"How could he have that kind of money if he was in prison for thirty years?"

Kamala replied,

"Just because his picture is in the newspaper that doesn't make him the killer and a thief, now does it Jeff?"

After Kamala and Jeff got to the police station, Jeff talked to the arresting officer about the old man they had in custody. He found out that Kamala's Grandpa was in prison for killing her Mother but he already severed his time. But her Grandpa was the thief too. They found out that he had stolen the money from a High Stakes Poker Game.

Kamala asked Jeff,

"How long of a time will he have to serve?"

Jeff replied,

"Oh, he'll probably will get ten years, I suspect!"

Jeff realized something and told Kamala,

"Kamala that seventy some year old man is not just your Grandpa, he is my as well."

What a sad moment for the two, they wept together. After he served three years of his prison term, he was out on parole for good behavior, but he lived on the streets and mind his own business. He was a Grandpa that neither one of them knew. But he got his clothing from...........

An Old Tub Of Clothing For The Homeless

and ate his meals in the homeless shelter. He died a few years after that. Kamala and Jeff found out about it when they found a newspaper that was lying around after he was already buried. What a sad moment for the two.

CHAPTER TWENTY-FOUR

It Was Fire-Engine Red

Kamala was getting tired of taking the bus when she had to go a long distance even though she loved to walk. She made a serious decision to purchase a car not just any car, she had her heart set on a station wagon with a radio that played the oldies but the goodies music, but it had to be fire-engine red in color she'd found one than she bought it. Kamala had to learn to drive, so she did. When it was time to take her fire-engine red station wagon out it was available.

One morning Kamala decided to take off in her brand new wagon, she took a drive to Cincinnati and followed the Ohio River up through the scenic route it was more beautiful than what she even thought. After she had driven about 100 miles she started thinking it would be best for her to go back home; she did. She was tired when she returned back home but she was a good tired.

A few weeks later Kamala made another major decision to sell her red-brick home to buy a place out in the country. She took her fire-engine red station wagon out then followed route 50 it was very curb but she was fine with that. She drove until she got to a small town called Owensville. She stopped long enough to have a cola and a cheeseburger loaded [put through the garden]. While she was there, she picked up a classified ad newspaper then read it until she came to the ads for farms for sale.

Kamala kept reading until she came across a farm for sale that had fifty acres of land in a small town called Afton. It read it had a variety of fruit trees, fruit bushes, and the land was well cultivated from previous farmers. She asked around about its location; she was given directions to the farm she found it was near a much larger town called Williamsburg.

Kamala droved herself until she came to this peculiar farm. When she got out of her station wagon there was this gentleman, he fell in love with her car he wanted to buy it she told him,

"It's not for sale sorry, but I am interested looking at your farm."

The gentleman showed Kamala around it had a huge black barn a farmhouse that had large rooms plus a summer kitchen [a place to do canning during the harvest time]. She told herself,

"This would be a very nice place to raise a family."

Kamala had ideas to change the old black barn into a Family Style Restaurant. She told herself,

"I can feed the family there for sure. This would be a place to make money; plus, I can write true stories about the things that might happen here it sounds great to my thinking."

Kamala told the farmer she loved the place then she told him she was interested in buying the place.

After a few weeks, she sold her red-brick home, then she purchased the farm. She had plenty of money to start fixing things she had in mind, like a gathering table that would seat at least 16 people at the same time along with other dinette tables that would surround the fire-place she would have built. There were many things to be done to get the restaurant up and running. She put all she had into the place to get it open.

Kamala felt real satisfied about what she had planned and had done so far to the place. She told herself,

"I can teach the youngsters to write, read, and some math plus I can teach them how to cook almost anything."

All of this brought joy to Kamala's heart to have; have a houseful of children when the time would come around. She continued what she had started thinking,

"This place will be a rewarding life for all the children and myself too."

Kamala's thoughts still rambled on,

"The youngsters and I can plant an enormous vegetable garden right here for ourselves and our customers that we will have in time. We can do a lot of canning with the vegetables and fruit, during harvest time I think that would be fun and educational. Just think we can have plenty of fruit pies, cobblers or use the fruit for just plain eating. Not just that we can make many of meals with vegetables alone."

Kamala put all her energy into the place day by day. After a few months, she got married to a real nice man; then she had a little girl with reddish brown hair like hers. The couple named her Leha Ann. That's the story about.

It Was Fire-Engine Red.

CHAPTER TWENTY-FIVE

What's Going On?

Kamala found out that she couldn't have any more children. She was sad with that kind of news. Leha Ann has feel her heart with much joy but Kamala wanted to have a house full of children. Leha Ann over heard that her Mother couldn't have any more children when she was in the doctor's office with her Mother. This even saddened Leha Ann because she knew how much her Mother wanted more children. Not just that Leha was almost grown.

At a much later time, Leha Ann was reading the evening newspaper about where a couple was in a very bad car accident. The couple didn't survive the accident. The couple had 15 children ranging from the age of 15 years old down to the age of 2 months old. She followed the story for weeks.

Leha Ann was reading the newspaper one evening when her Mother mentioned to her,

"Leha Ann, I had no idea that you even read the newspaper, what's going on? What has made you so interested in reading the paper anyway?"

Leha Ann responded seriously,

"Mother! I have been following this story about this couple had a very bad car accident and they didn't survive it and right here Mother the paper says the children had no other living relatives and that they would be put into the Cincinnati Children's Home to be adopted out. Mother, there were 15 children ranging from the age of 15 years old and on down to the age of two months."

Kamala looked at Leha Ann and asked her seriously,

"Leha Ann, what makes you so interesting about this story?"

Leha Ann replied,

"Well, Mother the story caught my eye right after I overheard what the doctor told you, about......."

she stopped, her Mother said,

"About what Leha Ann?"

Leha Ann replied,

"Not being able to have...."

Kamala said,

"Children?"

Leha Ann responded,

"Yes! Mother!"

Kamala seriously said,

"What are you wanting me to do Leha Ann, take care of these children?"

Leha Ann responded,

"Mother, why are you so bitter?"

Kamala replied,

"No Leha Ann, I'm not bitter, I feel for these youngsters, Leha Ann you're the same age as the oldest child, if it was you, I would be there in no time at all, but there's 15 here!"

Leha Ann asked,

"Mother, you've said many times that you wanted a houseful of children, now it's your chance Mother."

Kamala thought for a few minutes on this situation. Leha Ann said,

"Mother what are you waiting for, here are your children!"

While pointing at the newspaper column.

Leha Ann said,

"Mother, what's going on?"

CHAPTER TWENTY-SIX

Seriously Split-Up The Youngsters Nay!

Kamala started thinking seriously about the 15 homeless children and about the time when she was raised by strangers. She didn't want this to happen to them but of course, Kamala would be a stranger at first but she just knew in her heart she wouldn't let this occur very long with these youngsters.

One evening when the newspaper came Leha Ann went out to get it; it wasn't there she called to her Mother, anxiously

"Mother! What has happened to the newspaper?"

Her Mother replied,

"Leha Ann, I have it why?"

Leha Ann didn't hesitate for one second longer she went to the kitchen right where her Mother was reading the newspaper. Leha Ann saw that her Mother was reading about the youngsters and asked her Mother seriously,

"Mother, are you going to make a home for the youngsters?"

Kamala looked at her daughter with a smile on her face. Kamala said anxiously,

"I'll do my best Leha Ann!"

Leha Ann jumped for joy for the youngsters but her Mother told her,

"Leha Ann, remember Mother can't make a promise but what I can do is...."

she stopped. Leha Ann anxiously said,

"Mother, you're the best mother that any child would want Thank You!"

Kamala replied to that statement,

"Don't thank me yet because we haven't got the youngsters as yet."

Kamala made a telephone call to the children's services first and told them who she was and what her intentions were about the 15 youngsters. She was told she would have to go to the court house to purchase licenses first then she would have to fill out an application and she had to qualify too.

Kamala didn't want the chance to loose those children because she wanted to be their parent. She knew she couldn't take the place of their Mother but she could provide for them with a home where they would be loved and cared for.

After Kamala had done all that would qualify her as the parent or guardian, she was granted custody of the 15 youngsters. It was a long process but the Children's Home wanted to split the youngsters up Leha Ann told her Mother while shaking her head no,

"Seriously split-up the youngster's nay!"

Kamala anxiously uttered,

"Now Leha Ann first let's go to the Children's Home to see what we can do to prevent this of not happening!"

When Kamala and Leha Ann arrived at the Children's Home all 15 youngsters were holding hands neither one wanted to be split up. Kamala started looking at the youngsters like they were hers already. Kamala talked to the lady in charge about the situation. After she took a look at the case not too awful long after that the lady in charge told Kamala,

"Kamala the youngsters; all fifteen of them are yours to have!"

When Kamala and Leha Ann heard that the two walked over to the youngsters and held out their arms to welcome them into their life. Kamala and Leha Ann anxiously responded,

<u>"Seriously Split-Up The Youngsters Nay!"</u>

CHAPTER TWENTY-SEVEN

The Middle Child

Kamala made the youngsters feel welcome in her farmhouse but Chantel the eight year old [which is known as the middle child] seemed to be sad most of the time. Leha Ann tried many things to make her happy. Nothing seemed to be working, no matter what she did. Chantel made the sun and the moon her friends.

When the sun or moon didn't appear because the sky was filtered with clouds all day long; Chantel felt more than sad she would curl-up her body and cry herself to sleep. This even made Kamala and Leha Ann sad. Kamala thought to herself,

"Just maybe, if I let Chantel tell me what was her favorite food I could fix it just for her."

Kamala went to Chantel that afternoon and asked her,

"Chantel if I cooked your favorite food what would that might be?"

Chantel just stared at Kamala with a sad face she didn't utter one single word or sound. Kamala decided to ask the oldest youngster Bob the fifteen-year-old,

"Bob, can you tell me what I can do? To make Chantel happy, what is her favorite kind of food?"

Bob replied,

"Peanut-Butter and Jelly, that's her favorite kind of food of all food."

Kamala went to the kitchen to fix Chantel a Peanut-Butter sandwich for the eight-year-old but she asked her,

"Chantel now tell me what is your favorite kind of Jelly?"

Chantel anxiously said with that toothy smile,

"Blackberry!"

Kamala was in luck once she spread on the Blackberry Jelly over top of the Peanut-Butter and put the other slice of bread on it. Chantel gave Kamala a big smile and then ate her sandwich. She told Kamala after she had finished eating,

"Thank you, Kamala, for my sandwich it was delicious now you can be my best friend forever!"

This made Kamala happy too, to know that she made

The Middle Child

Chantel was happy as well.

CHAPTER TWENTY-EIGHT

The Youngsters Was Told They Could Pick Out What They Wanted

Kamala was instructed by the Children's Home that the youngsters would be coming there twice a year for their garments. Time came to go on their first trip Leha Ann helped her Mother to put the youngsters into the Fire-Engine Red Station Wagon.

After they arrived at their destination the youngsters were told they could pick out the clothing they wanted. The clothing was in binds by size and the boys and girl's clothes were separated in different binds. There was a large assortment of clothing to choose from.

This was something new to the youngsters to have their clothing be provided by the Children's Home. The youngsters face looked kind of puzzled. When the youngsters started looking through the binds nothing seemed to match, no matter what they picked up. The older youngsters helped the younger ones, then the older ones went rummaging through the binds to choose what they might wear. Kamala and Leha Ann saw how much trouble they were having to find something to pick for their own selves. Kamala and Leha were thinking the same thing,

"These youngsters didn't ask for this situation, it was very disturbing to see them rummaging through the binds but this was a situation that couldn't have been helped."

Kamala saw the sadness that came across their faces when they started to leave so she turned their sad face to smiles when she told the youngsters she would help all she could to fit them up to balance out what they had chosen to wear. On their way home Kamala stopped at the creamy whip and looked at the youngsters and…….

They Were Told They Could Pick Out What They Wanted.

CHAPTER TWENTY-NINE

His Friends Couldn't Be Seen By The Naked Eye

Tommy the seven year old started rummaging through his clothes he had got from the Children's Home and asking someone or something while holding them up,

"Do you like this?"

Kamala looked at Tommy with a questionable face and asked,

"Tommy, who are you talking to?"

Tommy anxiously said,

"My friend!"

Kamala asked him,

"Who is your friend Tommy?"

Tommy replied while pointing in the air,

"You can't see him, he's standing right there?"

Kamala anxiously said,

"Why not Tommy, I can't see your friend."

Tommy held up some more clothes and looked in another direction and asked,

"Do you like this?"

Kamala anxiously said,

"Do you have another friend, Tommy?"

Tommy replied,

"Yes!"

Kamala was told by Leha Ann,

"Mother, **His Friends Couldn't Be Seen By The Naked Eye!"**

She replied,

"Why not Leha Ann?"

Leha Ann responded,

"Because his friends are in his imaginary world."

Kamala reminded herself.

"Oh, how dumb could I be, after all, I wrote over twelve hundred fairytales in my life time what was I thinking, I wasn't?"

CHAPTER THIRTY

The Surprise Was Tightly Tucked In Her Fist

KAmle, the six year old and Panya, the five year old stucked together like two peas-in-a-pod. One particular sunny day Leha Ann was playing hide-in-seek-and-find with the two. Leha Ann couldn't convince them to separate from one another. So, there wasn't much competition among one another.

After a few minutes, the other youngsters joined in with them. Leha Ann loved to play games with the youngsters. This brought joy to Kamala's heart seeing how much fun they all were having especially running after squirrels up the trees and running rabbits across the lawn and watching the deers nibbling the soy-beans that were planted near the woods.

Well, when it was time to go in for super Leha Ann would help gather up the youngsters. After counting heads there were two missing Kamel and Panya. The youngsters and Leha Ann looked high and low for them. Bob, the fifteen-year-old felt like it was his thought that they were missing. Leha Ann tried to convince him by telling him,

"Bob calm down we'll keep looking they are bound to be found, the little tikes must be around somewhere all of us are in this together."

Leha Ann told the youngsters to go on inside; they did. Then Leha took a walk down the Rooty road that went from the main high-way to the farm-house. She looked under the brush for a few minutes she couldn't see them anywhere. Leha was feeling franticly because she couldn't find the little blonde headed tikes.

A few minutes went into a half-hour, then the six-year-old came popping out, and then not too long after the five-year-old from the same area where her sister appeared. Leha asked them,

"What are you two doing down by the road, don't you know you could have been hurt?"

Their little round faces looked scared; it was like Leha scolded them. The two started sobbing together, then Leha took the two by their hands while the other one was hiding behind their back when Leha Ann arrived back at the house with the little tikes and took them inside everybody was relieved that they were safe.

Leha Ann asked the six-year-old,

"Kamel, what are you hiding behind your back?"

Kamel thought she would be in trouble if she showed Leha Ann what she had said sadly,

"Flowers."

Leha Ann asked the five-year-old the same question she asked the six-year-old,

"Panya what are you holding behind your back?"

Panya thought the same thing that her sister did and said sadly,

"Flowers."

When the two brought their hands out from their back the two had a bouquet of tiger lilies; the tigerish flowers blended right in with the color of their attire.

The Surprise Was Tightly Tucked In Her Fist, from the six year old. **The Surprise Was Tightly Tucked In Her Fist,** from the five year old. Leha Ann assured the two they weren't in trouble and told the tikes gently not to go down the Rooty road alone. That's the story about......

The Surprise Was Tightly Tucked In Her Fist.

CHAPTER THIRTY-ONE

The Dessert; For The evening, Which Was Lemon Meringue Pie

While the youngsters was eating their supper their bright eyes was eying **The Dessert; For The Evening Which Was Lemon Meringue Pie,** while setting around the gathering table. Jim, James, Cindy and Carol loved lemon meringue pie, and they were like four copy-cats and asked together; it sounded like there was an echo in the room,

"Is that lemon meringue pie we see?"

Kamala loved seeing the youngster's eyes lit up. She told the youngsters,

"Yes, that is lemon meringue pie but you have to eat your supper first and yes, the dessert is for the evening eating."

Jim the thirteen-year-old told James the eleven-year-old in his ear,

"Eat your peas or you won't get any pie."

Cindy the ten-year-old told Carol the nine-year-old in her ear,

"You better eat your potatoes or you won't get any pie."

Jane looked at all four with an evil eye and told them with her ten-year-old voice,

"That's not nice to whisper, if you got something to say; say it out loud!"

Kamala looked over at Jane and mentioned to her with a kind voice,

"Now Jane leave them alone, they aren't hurting anyone let me whisper they're only having fun. Why don't you join them at the gathering table until everyone is finished eating their supper?"

Jane went back at the table but not by her choice while puckering her face. Alice, the fourteen-year-old, told the youngsters,

"Now all of you better eat and quit playing with your food or noon will have pie."

After they all finished eating the youngsters excused themselves from the table then Alice, Bob, and James washed the dishes and cleaned the kitchen.

The Dessert; For The Evening Which Was Lemon Meringue Pie, had disappeared in no time at all but Lachele the four old, Joey the three year old, Benny the. two-year-old and Timmy the two-month year old fell to sleep before it was served. Leha Ann done up the dessert plates and silverware. Chantel, Tommy, Kamel and Panya didn't want....

The Dessert; For The Evening, Which was Lemon Meringue Pie.

CHAPTER THIRTY-TWO

What A Radiant Morning

What a radiant morning, the sky was free of clouds, the sun was shining and there was a gentle breeze blowing through the screen of an open window. Kamala remembered that the third Sunday in July was National Ice Cream Day.

While Leha Ann and the youngsters were pairing one another up to do the wheelbarrow race, Kamala started dicing, slicing, chopping, peeling, shredding, and mixing. what she needed for, to celebrate the National Ice Cream Day she called for the children to come in.

Bob the fifteen-year-old helped Leha Ann gather up the other fourteen youngsters. Bob called off their names as they came in.

Because he didn't want to have any of the youngsters missing if he could help it. Bob noticed that Lachele the four-year-old wasn't counted for.

Leha Ann and Bob the fifteen-year-old went looking for Lachele. Rain clouds started rolling in, the gentle breeze turned to a gust of wind. There were broken branches, loose leaves were flying through the air. As time went on, the sky was blackened by smokey looking clouds in no time at all. There were twigs propelling through the air then a clap of thunder echoed through the air, while uncontrolled lightning was striking across the wide-open space. Leha Ann and Bob were frightening for little Lachele.

Not too much later the rain came, the winds were wiping it across the land neither Leha Ann nor Bob could see beyond their eyes. Bob felt water around his paint's legs from walking through the creek that ran along the lower part of the land. Bob started calling for Lachele there were no words uttered from her after he called out her name several times.

After Bob started walking further down the creek his feet found an object when he picked it up he recalled it was a toy sailboat that he had given to Lachele. Leha Ann called for Bob. Bob heard her he told Leha Ann he was down by the creek. Bob just knew Lachele had drowned in the creek when he couldn't find her. Bob was panic-stricken by all of it. The rain had stopped Leha Ann found Bob; then not much longer Bob spotted Lachele near a tree lying on the ground. Bob and Leha Ann were relieved when he picked up Lachele in his arms her breathing was normal.

When the two showed up at the house with Lachele everybody cheered with much joy when they entered through the kitchen door. Kamala mentioned for all three to take a warm shower; they did. After the youngsters and Leha Ann gathered around the gathering table, Kamala and Leha Ann started scoping up the vanilla ice cream in bowls, then told the youngsters to top their ice cream with the summer berries of their choice and any other fruit she had prepared for the day.

Leha Ann, Bob, and Alice helped the younger youngsters, and then they did likewise for themselves. Before Kamala knew it, she was putting finishing touches with every bodies favorite sundae toppings. This was a welcome treat for the National Ice Cream Day for them all. That was the story about.......

What A Radiant Morning.

CHAPTER THIRTY-THREE

A Summer Birthday Bash

Kamala decided to have A Summer Birthday Bash for the youngsters because their birthdays was during the Summer months, plus it was Timmy's first birthday that very same day. Kamala loved to grill outside. While Kamala, Leha Ann and Alice done the dicing, slicing, chopping, pealing, stirring, shredding, and the mixing; for the food she was planning to make for the event, she told Bob and the other youngsters to pick out what games they would like to play.

The youngsters played horse-shoes, bean bag toss, and ring toss practically all day long, they stopped long enough to eat their Birthday Dinner, and their Birthday Cake. Kamala had some gifts for the youngsters not just gifts but personalized gifts such as handkerchiefs for the boys and hankies for the girls with their name's embroidered on them. The youngsters face showed an appearance of appreciation and by telling Kamala how generous she was and told her one by one,

"Thank You, Kamala!"

After fifteen thank you, Kamala was more than pleased with the youngsters in how well-mannered they were. That was the story about the day that Kamala threw together,

A Summer Birthday Bash.

CHAPTER THIRTY-FOUR

The Yellow Tablecloth

Leha Ann was very creative just like her Mother, she loved to draw and painted what she drew and her works were framed and put on display around the restaurant where people could admire them and the customers could purchase them too.

Leha Ann was looking through some material her Mother had laid away after she was finished with them. While rutting through the big tub of many colors of cloth she found one she liked it was yellow in color when she spread it out on the gathering table it fit to a tee.

Leha Ann wanted to write something on it that would be suitable for the whole family. She wrote out words, what a family does that would bring the family together often. One by one the youngsters asked Leha Ann,

"What are you doing Leha Ann?"

"Can I help?"

"What are you making?"

"Are you making something for us?"

"Are you making something for the table?"

"That's a pretty cloth you have Leha Ann, what are you going to do with it?"

"Leha Ann, I know what you're writing. You are looking for words to put on that yellow cloth, aren't you?"

"Leha Ann, I know what you can write on your yellow cloth, do you want me to tell you?"

"Leha Ann I have a great idea."

"Can I write something?"

"Let me write Leha Ann."

"Me too."

"Let me write."

"I can do it, let me."

"Let me."

After all the youngsters asked questions, Leha Ann knew what to print on,

The Yellow Tablecloth.

The words she decided on, she printed them and embroidered them on the yellow cloth of her choice, it read.........

The Family that Prays Together Stays Together was suitable for the whole family.

CHAPTER THIRTY-FIVE

Dicing, Slicing, Chopping, Pealing, Shredding and Mixing Vegetables

One morning Kamala wasn't feeling well so Leha Ann told her Mother she would get things ready for the day at the restaurant After Leha Ann had done the dicing, slicing, chopping, peeling, stirring shredding, and mixing, a peculiar man stepped into the kitchen where Leha Ann was preparing for the afternoon meal. She couldn't tell if he was a tramp or a clown because his attire looked kind of different.

Leha Ann just stood...and stared at him for a few minutes then she asked the man,

"Can I help you sir?"

He replied by saying with a rough voice,

"I'm hungry young lady, what do you have to eat!"

Leha Ann gave the man some raw vegetables she just prepared and told him,

"Sir, that's all I have for now, will that do?"

The man responded,

"But Madam have no money that I can give you."

Leha Ann told the man,

"That's ok, just eat."

He looked at Leha Ann for the longest time, he had a fierce look about himself. Something told Leha Ann she was up against a

105

challenge dare when the man picked up a sharp knife. Leha Ann picked up one herself.

Before she knew it the two were dancing around while sweeping the air with their knives. Leha Ann was blinded by the sun light that appeared through the window that was just above her head. She was cut off guard when the man swiped his knife through the air. His blade could have pierced her shoulder, but she switched to another position, and with a swinging movement, she was able to swipe his face with her knife.

The man dropped his knife and ran out the door, while his face was bleeding and dripping blood on his way out. Leha Ann told herself out loud,

"He'll regret that he even came in here."

Bob stepped into the restaurant and followed the trail of blood, he asked Leha Ann, with a serious voice,

"What's going on Leha Ann? Why is there blood dripping on the floor, are you alright?"

Leha Ann told Bob what just happened. He said anxiously,

"Leha Ann, you could have been killed!"

Leha Ann said with assurance,

"I know, but I'm not."

Bob saw the fear in Leha Ann's face and took hold of her by his arms and held her like he was fearful for her life. He held Leha Ann close to his chest. She felt his concern, then she started to cry. Bob put his hand across Leha Ann's head, then he pushed her head close to his heart then he held her for the longest time to comfort her.

Leha Ann remembered what she needed to do and pulled away from Bob, then bagged everything up, then filled the empty containers of the raw vegetables she had diced, sliced, chopped, peeled, and shredded, then she put the rest in the walk-in-cooler for reserved.

CHAPTER THIRTY-SIX

Who Was That Man; What Did He Want?

Leha Ann decided to go to the restaurant by herself the next morning; earlier than the day before. Something told her she shouldn't of because of what had happened the day before. Leha Ann wanted to make some fruit pies before it got too hot and add them to the menu.

After Leha Ann finished dicing, slicing, chopping, peeling, stirring, shredding, and mixing, she bagged everything up and filled the empty containers of what she did, then she put the rest in the walk-in-cooler for reserved except for the extra apples, peaches, and mangoes which was to be used for the pies.

After Leha Ann was finished she stepped into the dining area to make sure the gathering table and the other dinette tables had plenty of silverware and extra napkins because of adding the pies to the menu. She was startled suddenly when she saw a peculiar man standing in the door-way. She started to scream at first but instead, she asked herself,

"Now who is that man what does he want and how did he get inside in the first place?"

The man introduced himself by saying,

"By the way mama my name is Roy and your Leha Ann right?"

Leha Ann didn't know what to say she just stood there in a frozen state. She finally got the nerve to ask the man,

"Who are you? Now what do you want with me and by the way, how did you get inside and how is it that you know my name?"

The man held out his hand to shake Leha Ann's but instead, she decided to scream and when she did, she screamed hysterically hoping that someone would hear her. He assured her by saying,

"Now young lady you didn't need to do that, I'm not here to hurt you, Leha Ann."

Leha Ann asked him,

"Then why are you here?"

He replied,

"You know me when I tell you why I came here."

Suddenly she said,

"Well go ahead tell me, what's stopping you?"

He responded.

"First of all, Leha Ann like I told you my name is Roy, I have driven over 300 miles to apologize to you."

Leha Ann asked the man with a sharp tongue,

"For what?"

He answered,

"I have been in prison for ten years waiting to get out to tell you how sorry I am for...."

He stopped, Leha Ann asked him anxiously,

"For what?"

He replied,

"I'm the person that robbed your parents for money?"

She asked the peculiar man, with a bitter voice,

"Money for what?"

Roy replied,

"Because I was tired of being without."

Leha Ann questioned him,

"Why, were you hungry or what?"

Roy replied,

"Hungry for one and being homeless too."

Leha Ann mention,

"My Father is dead but my Mother is ill right now. Did you think to ask them for something to eat and a place to live? By the way, where are you living now, and are you hungry? Oh, well you said you have driven over 300 miles to get here to apologize, didn't you? ·"

Roy answered her by saying,

"First of all, I'm hungry for sure, second of all I do need a place to live, plus of course."

He stopped then Kamala stepped inside and had a puzzled look

Leha Ann,

"What is that man wanting Leha Ann?"

Leha Ann replied,

"Mother this man says he owes you apologies."

She replied,

"For what and who is he by the way?"

Roy stepped forward and helped out his hand to Kamala and started to shake her hand but she didn't respond he said,

"By the way my name is Roy. I'm here to tell you how sorry I\'m am for what I have put you and your husband through ten years ago. I have been in prison for ten years for robbing you and by the way I\'m sorry for your loss, but can you or will you accept my apologies, I could use some food and a place to live."

Kamala just took it all in, then asked Roy,

"How about a job and something to eat, plus a place to live?"

Roy anxiously answered Kamala by saying,

"Doing what, because I'm ready to start right now, madam"

Kamala answered,

"First let's get you something to eat."

Kamala gave Roy a cold cut sandwich and a salad and a piece of Leha Ann's peach and mango pie. While he was eating, Kamala asked Roy,

"How about you being Leha Ann's body-guard and living in the farm-house with us, but you got to know it's kind of crowded right now, but I believe we can find enough room for one more?"

Leha anxiously said, and thinking about Bob

"But Mother, I can take care of myself, please!"

Kamala replied,

"What is it dear, I understand you have had some indication of facing a peculiar man, and if it wasn't for Bob I wouldn't of know now; how long young lady were you going to keep that incident away from me?"

Leha Ann said anxiously,

"Mother, you have been under the weather lately so I left you alone, I'm old enough to choose, who can be my body-guard, Mother!"

Kamala asked,

"Who might that be young lady?"

Leha Ann replied,

"Bob, that's who, Mother."

Kamala replied,

"Roy will be your body-guard and that's that, and he can stay at the farm-house with the rest of us."

Leha Ann replied to her Mothers words,

"Mother! I won't like it and I know I can't go against what you had just said."

Roy stepped in front of Kamala and gave her a hug to thank her for everything she had offered him. Roy planned to keep his distance from Leha Ann so he wouldn't be oblivious, and no one would suspect anything. But Leha Ann went to Bob secretly and asked him behind her Mother's back,

"Bob, my Mother has the idea that I need a body-guard, and my Mother wants a stranger to be my body-guard will you be my bodyguard and keep Roy away from me? I would appreciate it Bob if you will!"

Bob seriously. asked her,

"What has happened Leha Ann? Has someone tried to hurt you again?"

Leha Ann replied,

"No Bob, no one had tried to hurt me. I was just startled suddenly by someone that my parents had encountered with, over ten years ago. Boy, you will be my body-guard, won't you; you don't have to tell anyone that I had asked you ok, Bob?"

Bob took Leha Ann by his hands and put his arms around her and told her with anxious voice,

"Of course, I will Leha Ann, and nobody will even expect anything that I am even around, except you Leha Ann."

Bob asked Leha Ann with a serious question,

"What about Kamala?"

Leha Ann assured him,

"Mother doesn't need to know Bob; can I count on you being my body-guard?"

Bob replied as he took hold of Leha Ann in his arms and said,

"Leha Ann I'll be there with bells on."

Then Leha Ann looked up at Bob with a gleam in her eyes, and Bob held her close to him and the two kissed. And neither one asked,

<u>Who Was That Man? What Did He Want?</u>

CHAPTER THIRTY-SEVEN

"Mother, Please I Was Just Picnicking With A Friend!"

Leha Ann took out the old iron skillet and fried up some chicken, baked beans, mashed potatoes, slaw, and made a blackberry pie. Bob just happened to step into the kitchen, Leha Ann was hoping he would. The first thing he asked,

"Is that fried chicken I smell?"

Leha Ann responded,

"Yes, it is Bob, I was hoping you would show up."

Bob replied,

"Why is that Leha Ann?"

Leha Ann answered,

"Bob, how about you and I go on a picnic?"

Bob responded,

"Sounds like fun Leha Ann, what about Kamala; What would she say?"

Leha Ann answered,

"What can she say?"

Bob replied,

"Where are you planning to have this picnic, Leha Ann?"

Leha Ann surprisingly said, while packing up the picnic basket,

"On the other side of the creek, it's private there; we won't be bothered there by anyone."

As Leha Ann and Bob started walking out the door Leha Ann picked up a red and white checkered board tablecloth, Bob carried the basket. When they reached their destination Leha Ann spread out the tablecloth Bob put the basket down on the corner of it. Bob started taking out the food but, Leha Ann asked Bob,

"What's the hurry, Bob?"

Bob just looked at Leha Ann with a puzzled face, Bob said,

"Is there something wrong Leha Ann?"

Leha Ann replied,

"Why no Bob, let's set a while first before eating, it will keep."

Bob said,

"Sure, it will."

In a few seconds, Bob put his arms around Leha Ann, she had that gleam in her eyes then Bob held her much closer and the two kissed several times.

Before the two went much further Leha Ann and Bob suggestive together,

"I think it would be best for the both of us is, to stop."

They did, then the two said together,

"I think it would be best for us is, to eat that fried chicken."

After they finished eating the two cleared the area and started walking back to the house. When the two walked inside, Kamala was staring at Leha Ann with a questioning face, and told Leha Ann,

"Young lady, go to your room."

She did, then Kamala followed her and asked her,

"What have you and Bob been up to, huh? Leha Ann, it would be best that you tell me the truth."

Leha Ann replied seriously,

"Seriously, Mother! Please I Was Just Picnicking With A Friend!"

CHAPTER THIRTY-EIGHT

She Was Engaged In Doing Her Daily Routine

Leha Ann received a telephone call from the Cincinnati University Hospital that her Mother was in the Intensive Care Unit because she was in a horrible car accident while she was engaged in doing her daily routine working at the Family Style Restaurant and playing with the younger youngsters.

When Leha Ann heard that news she dropped the receiver of the telephone on the floor. The news was devastating Leha Ann feel to her knees and placed her hands across her face and started tapping her face with her fingers the habit she picked up from her Mother and started sobbing Roy rushed over to her right that second Bob intervene and pushed Roy aside than took hold of Leha Ann and asked her,

"What's going on Leha Ann!"

Leha Ann kept sobbing while Bob helped her then he helped her to the nearest chair then she looked up at him with a frighten look about herself, she told Bob with a serious voice,

"Mother has been in a horrible car accident Bob!"

Bob replied,

"How bad is she Leha Ann?"

Leha Ann responded slowly,

"Shhhheee could die any minute Bob!"

Roy asked,

"Where is she Leha Ann, I'll take you there where ever she is!"

Leha Ann had no other choice but Roy, then told him,

"Thanks, Roy, she's at the University Hospital in Cincinnati."

Then she told Bob,

"Bob, you come along too, I need you there if you will?"

Bob replied,

"Of course, I will Leha Ann you know that I will, let's go now before it's too late!"

After they reached their destination, Leha Ann, Bob, and Roy went straight to the ICU looking for Leha Ann's Mother. Leha Ann went to the service desk to ask what room her Mother was in, the lady told her,

"I'm sorry young lady, your Mother has passed away."

Leha Ann started to ask the lady where was her Mother, instead, he felt nausea. Then she ran while holding her mouth looking for the nearest ladies room.

Bob went looking for Leha Ann when he found her, she took a deep breath, then let it out and told him while crying,

"Bob, Mother's gone, now what do I do, this can't be happening to us, we.... can't loose her. She's all I have, I mean she is all we have for a Mother!"

Bob put his arms around her, then the two cried together, what a sorrowful moment for the two. Roy went looking for the two after a few minutes he found them then he sat down nearby. When Bob and Leha Ann looked around, they saw Roy, then she told the men,

"It's best that we get going back home because there is nothing we can do here."

The trip back home was quiet, among them all. When they got home Leha Ann called for the rest of the youngsters to come to the living room. When they arrived, she told them sadly, while she sat in her Mother's Ricky rocking chair, but she tried not to cry any tears,

"Kamala is not with us any more youngsters, I'm sorry to say."

This was a very intense moment for them because they all loved Kamala very much. That afternoon,

She was Engaged In Doing her Daily Routine.

CHAPTER THIRTY-NINE

Fill In The Empty Space

After Leha Ann and the fifteen youngsters had told Kamala "Good-Bye"; She picked up the Family Bible off the stand that sat in the corner. Then she seated herself on the old Rickey rocking chair, where her Mother sat to read it. She opened it to the pages where the Family Records were written, then started reading it.

When she came to the page where her parent's names, Date of Birth were filled in. Her Father's Date of Death was already recorded by her Mother. But now it was time to fill in the empty space for her Mother's Date of Death.

This was something that Leha Ann wasn't up to, but it was time to fill in the empty space. Leha Ann laid her hands on the Bible. Then she stared at the empty space for the longest time, before even thinking about picking up the ball-point [pen] which had a goose feather attached to it which was pink in color.

Leha Ann felt she was robbed of her Mother because of the reckless driver. She felt like she was left alone to look after things especially the youngsters her Mother had taken in when she was more than half-grown herself. Leha Ann felt she was somewhat of a parent to them because she helped her with the fifteen youngsters. Leha Ann would do anything in this world to look after them. Leha Ann recalled the article in the newspaper about the youngsters loosing their parents because of a very bad car accident.

Leha Ann decided she was ready to pick up the ball-point[pen]. Her Mother would use to write in the Family Bible to record things like what she was left up to do. To Fill In The Empty Space of her

Mother's Date of Death. Leha Ann felt fatigued; cold after she had finished. Therefore, before she threw her Mothers colorful quilt over her shoulders she saw that she was surrounded by all fifteen youngsters.

They were holding one another hands just like the time when she and her Mother went to the Children's Home to pick them up and became a large part of their family.

Leha Ann remembered the yellow tablecloth she had made, then she asked the youngsters,

"Can anybody join this gathering?"

All fifteen said together with anxious voices,

"You can Leha Ann!"

She stood up, then took a hold of Bob's hand. then she took hold of Timmy's hand, then she asked them kindly,

"Bow your heads."

They did; she did likewise. Leha Ann said a prayer to ask the Heavenly Father to give them strength and courage through the coming days ahead because losing Kamala was a huge loss to the youngsters and Leha Ann too. Afterward, she repeated the words she had written, and embroidery on the yellow table-cloth which was,

"The Family That Prays Together, Stays Together."

They did. This concludes the story about Kamala Rae Waits.

Book Two

CHAPTER ONE

Nudging

This wasn't Jeff's usual morning routine because something was shoving him in going outside to get a newspaper that had been lying in the drive-way for several weeks after it had turned yellow in color. After he opened the door, all of a sudden he felt like he was pushed out into the brisk air.

Jeff's eyes were cast upon his surroundings to see if anyone was watching him, or no one. He dug up the paper from under gravel then he shoved off the dirt from the faded orange plastic sleeve. He felt like he was rushed back inside. Jeff laid the paper on the end-table that sat next to his lazy-boy chair.

Jeff left the area then he started all over on his regular routine by putting on a pot of caffeine coffee. At that moment, he took a bath, showered, and got dressed for the day. Jeff moved himself to the kitchen. He served himself a fresh cup of brewed coffee, then he seated himself at the kitchen table.

Jeff felt like something was nudging him he had naught one clue what could be so important in having his morning disturbed. He was getting annoyed by this, He went for his second cup of hot steaming coffee. Jeff felt like he was being strongly kicked back into the living-room. His eyelashes lead him over to his empty chair.

Jeff mentioned to himself while eyeing the mutilated paper that he wasn't planning on reading in the first place. He bought it to help a neighbor young-fellow, so he could join his friends at camp,

"To my wonder, I'm thinking there could be an article that I might need to read for some unknown reason!"

1

Jeff interrupted his thoughts when he poured himself the third cup of coffee. In a few seconds, the nudging started again, he thought,

"Now this nudging is getting ridiculous What could be in that paper that I need to know?"

Jeff shifted himself back to the living-room. He sat his hot cup of coffee down on the end-table while his eyes were eyeing the rolled paper. He seated himself in his chair and he picked up the paper, then he unrolled it carefully it smelt old.

The bold headlines seemed to jump off the page; he was devasted by what he had read. Jeff felt like the news he just read had to be a misprint. He crumpled up the paper, then he threw it across the room beyond his reach.

Jeff read the date on the top page it was telling him by this date on the calendar, Kamala had already entered into her resting place. Jeff wasn't ready to accept the sad news. He pointed himself directly down the hall to the bedroom Kamala had before she sold it to him.

Before he entered the room, he could still smell the fragrance of her perfume she wore, it filtered the air. Jeff started feeling drowsy. He scuffled his way over to her bed, he fell into it. He cuddled up with the colorful comfort she had left behind. His thoughts of her started destroying his mind, then he rolled over.

Jeff went into hibernating like a bear would on any winter session for several days. Jeff was soggily in his own way; his thoughts smothered his thinking about Kamala, a loved one he couldn't erase. Jeff jumped up and yelled out of his sleep,

"Kamala Rae, wait! Why did you have to die on me!?"

Jeff couldn't sleep he helped himself to the kitchen. By Jeff being half-asleep, he put on a pot of Irish Coffee. When it started brewing, he realized what he had done. He took in a deep breath it inflated his nostrils. He started to throw it out, but instead, he said,

"Heaven's to betise I'm going to drink it anyway it can't hurt me no more than I'm already hurting!"

2

Jeff helped himself to a cup of Irish Coffee, then something told him to move speedily to the living-room, he sat his cup down on the end-table and seated himself in his lazy boy chair. The first thing he eyed was that old crumpled up paper that he had thrown and what things he and Kamala had learned about who they really were.

Jeff started dwelling on the time he and Kamala had drank a pot of Irish Coffee along with the whipped cream and all. He recalled when Kamala would cross her hand across her face, she would start tapping her face with her fingers. She used it to her advantage when she became nervous it was something she picked up from her Daddy.

Jeff drank the whole pot of coffee, then he fell to sleep soundly.

Jeff was woken by a nuisance nudge. He jumped up out of his chair like he was shot. Jeff refrained himself from the nudge, then he relocated himself over to the newspaper that had landed on the rocking chair that Kamala used quite often while taking it easy.

Jeff picked up the paper, then he turned to the page that read in bold lettering that read the obituary column. He found her name, date, time she was laid to rest, and the place: Williamsburg, Oh. Cemetery.

Jeff called the funeral home to find out what lot number she was. He found out about Kamala's daughter; Leha Ann. This was hurting Jeff even more because that was the name, he and Kamala were going to name their baby if it had lived. Jeff shook his head back and forth and screamed out as loud as his lungs could carry,

"No!"

Jeff reached into his thoughts and asked,

"Kamala, why wasn't I told anything about you and your baby!" He had no one to comfort him; he wept hard, then he fell asleep in her rocker, he was exhausted.

CHAPTER TWO

What Could I Loose By Not Going Or Gain By Going?

Jeff felt rough when he awaken from sleeping in that old rocking chair. He had two different thoughts scrambling through his thinking. While Jeff was doing his usual routine, he asked himself the first thought,

"What could I gain by going to the cemetery?"

And Jeff asked himself the second thought,

"What could I loose by not going to the cemetery?"

Jeff replied,

"Oh! Fiddlesticks, I don't know what I'm doing I can't even make a simple decision. I'm going because I have a lot on my mind to attend to when I get to Williamsburg!"

After Jeff catches the bus, after he settles down in his seat he asks,

"This is something I need to do for myself, I got to tell......" he was disturbed by the thought. Jeff was carrying a heavy burden by her death. Jeff took in a deep breath, then he relaxed. Jeff finished what he was saying,

"I got to tell Kamala "Good-Bye."

Jeff was too choked up to even to say her name again it was really wedged tightly in his throat. After he cleared his throat, he said,

"Kamala, Kamala, Kamala!"

When Jeff reached his destination, he walked all over the town until he found the Williamsburg Cemetery. Then he moved himself around the grounds with his head down and observed the lot numbers.

While Jeff was looking for Kamala's headstone, he noticed a young-lady lurking around a tree. He gasped for air when he saw she looked identical to what Kamala did with her long reddish-brown hair hanging down to her waist.

When she noticed him glaring, she got skittish, then she placed her hands across her face, then she started tapping her face with her fingers. This was way too freakish for Jeff. Jeff started going toward her, then he froze in place because he just knew she was Kamala.

The young-lady ran away. Jeff picked up his heels and ran to her. When he got too close, she screamed. Jeff called out,

"Kamala, it's me, Jeff. Come back here!"

The same image again appeared close to his eyes. He started walking toward her, then he called her name several times,

"Kamala, Kamala, Kamala!"

He thought he might be hallucinating when he saw her again. He shook his head in disbelief; it had to be Kamala.

The young-lady then realized it was her Uncle Jeff when she saw his face. Because she had seen his picture in photos that was in the large yellow envelope that was given to her Mother back when Kamala needed it. She went back towards him, slowly.

The young-lady glared at Jeff with a questionable face, then she asked,

"Is that you Uncle Jeff?"

Jeff was surprised when she asked him that. Jeff took a second look and noticed it wasn't Kamala because she looked much younger than her.

Jeff asked,

5

"Ok, young-lady you must be Leha Ann, Kamala's daughter. Am I right?"

Leha Ann asked,

"How is it that you know me?"

Jeff assured her,

"I just knew the minute I cast my eyes on your pretty face, you and Kamala could be twins. You two look so much alike!"

In a few seconds, Leha Ann then realized that her Uncle Jeff wasn't at the cemetery when her Mother was laid to rest. She apologizes,

"Oh, Uncle Jeff, you're here to see where..........."

her voice weakened. She started to weep hard. Jeff took hold of her, while tears ran down her sad face. Then reality set in on Jeff, the two wept together.

After the two composed themselves, then they stepped over to Kamala's grave-site. Jeff was astonished by the imprint of a garland wreath that was made of clover flowers. It was a very impression marking on her head-stone it brought Jeff into tears to his eyes because he knew the time, when him and Kamala joined one together themselves.

Jeff rested on his knees, then he knew her name by tracing it with his fingers, then he said while tears flooded his eyes,

"Good-Bye....my.... sister........ Kamala....I'll.... miss you for the rest of my life. I'll....see you....in heaven I.... L-O-V-E.............You!"

Jeff studied what he had just seen. Jeff felt restless Leha Ann noticed her Uncle Jeff fidgeting, she asked,

"You know, Uncle Jeff, a family that prays together, stays together. Can I say a prayer for the both of us?"

Jeff studied Leha Ann's face and said slowly,

6

"You.... surely can, Leha Ann!"

Leha Ann took hold of Jeff's hands while praying; something nudged at Jeff that made him feel something, but what? Before the two left, his touch from Leha Ann made him feel that he was her Father.

Jeff didn't want to leave Williamsburg until he found out. After Leha Ann was finished praying, Jeff looked at her with a serious questionable face, then he asked,

"Leha Ann, can I ask you a personal question?"

She looked at him with a concerned face, then she asked,

"What might that be, Uncle Jeff?"

Jeff waited for a few seconds, then he cleared his voice and asked,

"I get a feeling that you're my-----"

Leha Ann glared at her Uncle with a stern face. then she asks,

"Uncle Jeff what is it You're scaring me but go ahead I'm listening."

Jeff swallows real hard like he had something in his throat, than he asks,

"Leha Ann, I feel we are related in more than one-way. Could that be possible?"

Leha Ann questioned,

"How's that, Uncle Jeff?"

He replied,

"Well, child it's this way I have the odd feeling that you're my ...."

Leha Ann stared over at her Uncle then she asked,

"Uncle Jeff, what are you trying to tell me?"

Jeff finished,

7

"It's like this child Kamala wanted to name our baby the very same name that you have, child!"

Leha Ann was stunned by what she heard and said,

"But Uncle Jeff, you and Mother are brother and sister, so how could that be?"

Jeff felt he needed a different location to finish this conversation, he asks,

"Leha Ann, is there somewhere else we could go besides here?"

Leha Ann replied,

Of course, there is we can go to the summer-kitchen if that's ok with you, Uncle Jeff?"

Jeff asks,

"Is it within walking distance?"

Leha Ann replied,

"Yes, Uncle Jeff, so let's get away from here."

Before the two left the cemetery, they went back over to Kamala's grave-site, then they picked some clover flowers for her, then they left quietly.

Jeff and Leha Ann had mixed thoughts rambling through their head. After the two walked down the root-like road, Jeff noticed there was lots of room to roam on he asked,

"How many acres does this place have?"

Leha Ann replied,

"50 acres, Uncle Jeff. Why?"

He replied,

"I was just courteous."

When the two got to the summer-kitchen Lehn Ann let Jeff inside, then she went to the farm-house to get the large yellow envelope of Kamala's. It was filled with photos and her birth records, but she didn't have any knowledge to that fact. After she returned, she laid the contents on the gathering table. Jeff asks,

"Child, listen to me first to what I need to tell you before we dive into those pictures..........please."

Jeff continued,

"When your Mother and I first met, neither one of us even knew that we were kin of any kind until we found out that our Fathers were brothers when we thought we were cousins. Right after her Dad was laid to rest, that's when I found out that my Father was Kamala's too. That's when we realized we were sister and brother. By then, it was too late because Kamala was pregnant with our baby!"

He continued,

"We lost our baby after she felled and miscarriage. She told me if we had a boy she plain to name him Kevin and if it was a girl she was going to name her Leha Ann."

Leha Ann mentioned to her Uncle Jeff,

"Uncle Jeff that's a sad story."

Jeff remembered the reason why the two had the contents out in the first place

While searching through them, Leha Ann came across her birth-records and Jeff found a picture of Kamala and Leha Ann together right after she was born. The two were furnished with the information that the two had been wanting to find out.

After Jeff read what was written on it that Leha Ann's Father was Jeff. After Leha Ann read who her Father was from her birth-certificate, the two were beside themselves, but Leha Ann asked,

"Uncle Jeff I mean Daddy or what do I call you? This is too confusing."

9

Jeff and Leha Ann stared at one another and said while hugging,

"This can't be real, but it is!"

Leha Ann had another question, she asked,

"Now Uncle Jeff, who was the man that was supposed to be my Father? How could my Mother let me in thinking differently? What do I do now, Uncle Jeff I mean, Daddy? I don't know what to think. It all stinks?"

Jeff took a hold of Leha Ann and said,

"Young-lady, this is all new to the both of us. Let's just enjoy what we have at this moment."

Jeff continued,

"I asked myself before coming here."

"What could I loose by not coming or gain by going?!"

After that, Leha Ann and Jeff stood up, then after they embraced as each other was comfortable with the idea of what the two had learned they wept

About the Author

Daisy Mae Spoonamore, USA writer was born in the greater City of Cincinnati....Where The Tyler Davidson Fountain Square known as "The Genius Of Water" is downtown, and The Carew Tower overlooking the Ohio River. Daisy is the second oldest child of five children, actually in time there were six children, down the line. The five children were raised from pillar to post; in Ohio, and Kentucky, and ate poor man's gravy made of lard, flour, water, and no seasoning. And poor man's biscuits made of lard, flour, water and leavening other than yeast. Most meals were made from scratch. During her time as a young child, was treated for epilepsy until she was thirteen of age, by the Cincinnati Children\'s Hospital seen by Dr. Phenney. She and her siblings went to several schools, by the time she was in the 11th grade a student at Clermont Northeastern High School in Owensville, Ohio, this is where she meets the love of her life, {he was a foster child along with others) her Valentine Sweetheart and married him for almost 56 years. Then God called him home from having Bladder Cancer. The couple lived in Cleveland, Vermillion on the lake, then back to Cleveland, Newark, Thornport, Felicity, Williamsburg, back to Newark, Ohio. The couple was blessed with one son {Ron Jr.} two daughters (Debbie Ann and Sandra Mae) and seven grandchildren, and eighteen great grandchildren. Daisy had studied hair at 3-B School of Beauty in Newark, Ohio, and gotten her Cosmetology license in 1975.

And she worked at a family self-owner restaurant, the Feed Mill in Felicity, plus Daisy had a Novelty and Gift Shop, and her spouse became business partners along with others, until her health fell at the age of fifty-three. Much later the writer made a complete comeback in her Golden Years.

Daisy has participated her hand in writing poetry; while dealing with her health issues. Some of her work became songs. 1. What Would I Do Without Me, when the doctor thought she had MS but she was tested twice; both tests came out to be negative and was tested to see if she had water on her brain from the doctor at the Cleveland Clinic, which came out to be negative also. That song is on a CD called Hands Across American Vol.11.2. Emptiness Inside. 3. A Pogo Stick. Three of her works were published in three different poetry books 1. Home Where The Harvest Is.2.Reaching My Triump.3. Dreams. Daisy was awarded with a certificate from the World Publishing Company in Creative Writing Skills.

Daisy has participated her hand in Creative Writing along with other writers at the local Library in Williamsburg, Ohio. Plus, she has been awarded with a Diploma from the Strafford Career Institute after completing a Program in Creative Writing on July 27, 2015. Daisy feels that she was born to be a writer, a God given talent. Daisy also studied Writing for Children of different levels, in which she has written over three hundred children stories and added over three hundred pieces of art illustrations rather than drawings of pictures for clarification for the stories. After she finished, she was awarded a well-deserved Diploma. Plus, she had written a book of facts; This and That, That and This, and What Have You, the only thing she received was the book jacket because she was taken for several thousand $'s from the publishing company she was paying. All she said, was, chalk it up as an expensive experience.

Now, Daisy is handing over copies of a three-part sequel; Kamala, Jeff, and Veronica. For publication; to make her works into a masterpiece, that she will be proud of. She says writing is a privilege so let your works reach the **outer-most.**

Daisy has been living with her Son, Ronald and Daughter-in-law Karen for six and a half years, and has taken care of her in many wonderful ways. With the feeling of much respect and appreciation from Daisy Mae.

www.ingramcontent.com/pod-product-compliance
Lightning Source LLC
Chambersburg PA
CBHW071529100726
47908CB00004B/1330